CW00728466

365 DOLLS

CLD 21379

This edition published in 1999 for Colour Library Direct,
Goldalming Business Centre, Woolsack Way,
Godalming, Surrey, GU7 1XW

text: Francisca Frölich
illustrations: Christl Vogl
translation: Stephen Challacombe
editing: Deborah Fox
production: TextCase, The Netherlands
cover design: Ton Wienbelt, The Netherlands

ISBN 1-84100-235-6

365 DOLLS

Bedtime Stories for every day of the year

1 January

Alice's wish

Tomorrow it would be Alice's birthday. She would be four; old enough to go to school. Alice had known for a long time what she wanted for her birthday – she wanted a baby brother or sister. Every time her parents asked, "What do you want for your birthday?" she said, "A new baby." Mummy's tummy was quite big. Alice knew that there was a baby in it. But would the baby be born tomorrow?

2 January

Her own baby

The next morning, Alice woke up early. She blinked twice.
Then she got very excited. It was her birthday! Hooray! She was going to get what she had longed for – a new baby! The door opened.
Daddy and Mummy came in. They sung "Happy birthday..." and then gave Alice her present. She tore off the paper and there was her new present ... a baby doll.
"I'm afraid you'll have to wait a little bit longer for your real baby brother or sister Alice, but now you have your own baby!" laughed her parents.

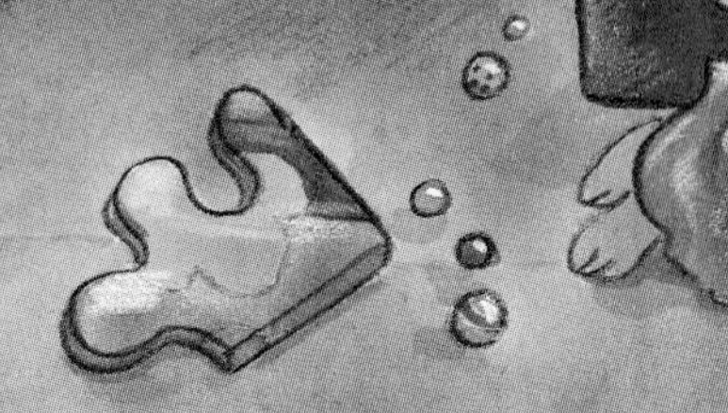

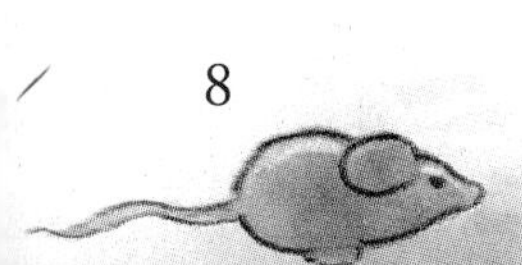

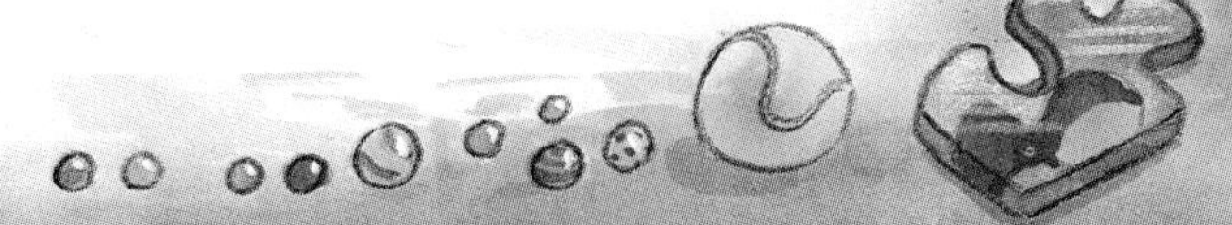

3 January

Practice

Alice was very happy with her new doll. She had wanted a real baby, but Daddy and Mummy had explained that babies are not delivered to order! Mummy was expecting a baby, but it would be a couple of months before her baby brother or sister would arrive. Until then she had to make do with her baby doll. Alice played with her new doll all the time. Grandma and Granddad had given her a baby's bottle, a potty and nappies. Her baby needed a new nappy every ten minutes.
"When your new brother or sister is born, you will be able to help us with everything," Daddy said to her with a big smile.
Alice nodded. "That's why I'm practising Daddy," she answered.

4 January

Think of a name

Alice was sitting on the sofa with her parents.
"Alice," asked Daddy. "Has your dolly got a name?"
"Oh no!" cried Alice. She had forgotten about a name. She would have to think what to call her doll. She liked the name Jack, but her doll was a girl, so she couldn't call her Jack. Maria? Amanda? Sarah? No, they just didn't seem right. The new name for her doll came to her in a flash.
"I am going to call her Diane," she said to her parents.
"Diane? That's a pretty name," said Mummy.

5 January

Winking

Diane was just as big as a real baby. She had blonde curls and blue eyes that closed when Alice laid her on her back.
"Now little girl," whispered Alice as she put Diane into her cot, "it's time for a nice rest." But Diane's eyes didn't close! Alice picked up Diane again and gently rocked her. One eye closed, but the other stayed open. Alice laughed. It looked so strange, just as though Diane was winking at her. Perhaps she was?

6 January **Bathtime**

Alice rolled up her sleeves. She had filled a big bowl with water because her doll needed a wash. She gently lifted Diane out of her cot and took off her clothes.
"There now Diane, I'm going to give you a bath," she said as she gently lowered the doll into the water. The water was cold. If baby dolls could shriek, Diane would have screamed the house down. She wasn't at all happy. How could Diane let Alice know that she wanted to get out of the cold water? Fortunately Alice's hands had got cold and so she lifted Diane out of the water.
"There, nice and clean again," she said as she dried the doll.
"Thanks, but no thanks," thought Diane. "No more baths ever again, please.
I will never get warm again!"

7 January

Favourite

Which of all Alice's dollies
Do you think she likes the best?
It's her baby doll called Diane,
She prefers to all the rest.

She combs her blonde and curly locks
And puts her in a clean new dress.
Like any proud new parent,
She is eager to impress.

The other dolls she quite forgets,
They are neatly put away.
Alice's thoughts are just on Diane,
Her favourite doll these days.

8 January

Abandoned

Since Alice had got her new doll, she had forgotten all about her other dolls. She left Rag Doll, Teddy Bear, Sally-Ann and Harlequin in the cupboard.
"I'm angry," said Rag Doll. "Alice never plays with us any more. It's just as though we don't exist."
"Yes I know," agreed Harlequin. "Thanks to that silly baby doll, Alice has just abandoned us."
Teddy Bear and Sally-Ann didn't say anything at all. They were sulking.

9 January

Don't be so mean

Rag Doll, Teddy Bear, Sally-Ann and Harlequin were angry with Diane the baby doll. They blamed her for the fact that Alice didn't play with them any more. That night they hissed at Diane. "You awful baby doll. Who do you think you are? Because of you, we have to spend the whole day in the cupboard."

Diane opened her big blue eyes. She was horrified. "Why are you so horrid?" she cried. "I can't do anything about it. Besides it's not much fun being a baby doll. Would you like being washed in freezing cold water? Or being pricked in the tummy by a pin whenever Alice puts a clean nappy on. It isn't much fun at all."

The others hadn't thought about that. Perhaps they had been a bit mean to Diane after all. "Can't we all be friends again?" asked Teddy Bear.

10 January

Peace at last

Rag Doll, Teddy, Sally-Ann and Harlequin had made friends with Diane. Rag Doll and Harlequin could be a bit difficult sometimes, but that was because Alice used to play with them the most. Now that Diane got all the attention, they were incredibly bored. Teddy was rather pleased to have some peace and quiet.
"I used to be cuddled so often," he muttered, "that my ears are practically falling off now and my left ear is just held on by a thin thread." Teddy felt much happier having more rests now.

11 January

Sally-Ann

Alice has had Sally-Ann for a long time. Some of Alice's old toys had been given away, but Sally-Ann was one of her favourites. Poor Sally-Ann had been bitten in the tummy by a toy crocodile Alice used to have. She was glad the crocodile had been given away. She was still proud though to show off her scars to her friends!

12 January

Raggy and Harry

Rag Doll and Harlequin were best friends. Harlequin called Rag Doll Raggy and Rag Doll called Harlequin Harry. Raggy and Harry looked a bit pitiful. Raggy's arms and legs hung limply from his body. Two large tears had been painted on Harry's cheeks. But really they were very happy dolls. They were both fond of telling jokes and they laughed a lot together. When Harry thought of a great new joke, Raggy went all droopy with laughter. And Harry's tears were really tears of laughter.

13 January

Friends

Do you know the dearest friends
Of Diane the baby dolly?
They live together in Alice's house
In the cupboard, in a trolley.

Harlequin and Sally-Ann,
Rag Doll and cuddly Teddy,
From now on they'll always be
There for each other at the ready.

14 January

Let's travel

"If Alice won't play with us, we must think of something that's fun to do," said Raggy the Rag Doll. "Hmm," muttered Teddy. "What could we do?"
"I have always wanted to travel," said Sally-Ann, "to have exciting new experiences."
"An excellent idea!" exclaimed Harry the Harlequin. "Where shall we go?"
"At least to another room," said Sally-Ann. "We've been here so long that we know every inch of the place."
"Yes, but ..." stammered Raggy. "It's easy for you to talk. But how am I going to walk that far with my limp legs?"
Oh dear, that would be a problem. Without Raggy, the others didn't want to go anywhere.

15 January

By taxi

What could they do? They were deep in thought. They wanted to travel, but Raggy just couldn't walk very far with his limp legs. Harlequin and Sally-Ann sighed. They didn't know what to do. Teddy closed his right eye. The other eye was loose and he couldn't close it.
"I know. We'll all go by taxi!" yelled Teddy.
"By taxi?" The other dolls were puzzled.
Teddy explained his plan. "Not a real taxi, but in Diane's pram. Alice often takes Diane out for a walk. If we hide on the rack underneath the pram, we will get a free ride from our room!"

16 January

A tight squeeze

Rag Doll, Harlequin, Sally-Ann and Teddy Bear crept silently under the pram. They all had to fit on the rack. There was barely enough room for all four of them to squeeze in together, but they managed it - just! Now they had to wait until Alice took Diane for a walk.
"Phew! It's taking so long!" grumbled Harry. "I've got cramp in my leg." He wanted to move and sit more comfortably, but there was no room on the rack.
He accidentally kicked Sally-Ann's tummy.
"Ouch!" she cried. "Watch out Harry."
"Ssshh! Be quiet! They'll spot us," warned Raggy.

17 January

An adventure

Alice lifted her baby doll out of her cot.
"Now little one, Mummy is going to take you for a walk," she said. She dressed Diane in clean clothes and carried her to the dolls' pram. Diane was looking forward to going for a walk. Before they left, she wanted to say hello to her friends Rag Doll, Harlequin, Sally-Ann and Teddy. She looked over to their cupboard but it was empty. Where were her friends? She heard a shuffling noise under the pram. What a surprise! There were her friends underneath the pram. "How wonderful," she thought, "we're all going off on an adventure together."

18 January **Bump, bump, bump**

Alice didn't know that Rag Doll, Harlequin, Sally-Ann and Teddy had hidden under the pram. They wanted to discover some new places. Alice crossed the landing and pushed the pram down the stairs ... bump, bump, bump ... the pram bounced over every step.
"Ouch, ouch!" shouted Harry, Raggy, Sally-Ann and Teddy. At last they reached the bottom of the stairs. What a relief!
"It's just as well dolls don't get bruises," sighed Raggy.

19 January **Going outside**

"What an adventure," gasped Sally-Ann. "If I had known we had to go downstairs," complained Rag Doll, "I would never have come. I am a complete wreck. We've been bumped and shaken over every step."
"Stop moaning," said Sally-Ann. "When you have an adventure, you have to expect some uncomfortable moments."
"Where do you think we will go?" asked Harry.
Teddy pointed with his paw. "Alice is walking towards the front door. Perhaps we are going outside."

20 January

White stuff

Alice pushed the pram outside.
Although it was the middle
of the winter, the sun was
shining. Alice pushed the
pram along the garden path.
"Hey, what's that stuff?"
asked Harlequin.
"It's really cold and wet!"
screeched Rag Doll. The white
"stuff" was snow. As the
wheels of the pram turned, they
spattered snow on to the four friends.
They were soon soaking wet and dirty.
"We're not going on any more travels!"
they grumbled. They wished they had stayed
indoors in their safe cupboard. At least it wasn't
cold and wet there!

21 January

What a journey!

The three dollies and cuddly Teddy
Are so eager and so ready
For adventure far and wide
So in the dolly's pram they hide.
But they really weren't prepared
For bump, bump, bumping down the stairs.
They were bumped and really shaken,
Then all through the front door taken.
Thc dirty snow from thc gardcn path
Means they all now need a bath!

22 January

Dirty dolls

Rag Doll, Harlequin and Sally-Ann looked very dirty.
But Teddy was the worst of all.
"I'm never going to stow away underneath a dolls' pram ever again," grumbled Raggy. Harry and Sally-Ann couldn't agree more. They never wanted to travel again. The world outside the children's room was full of horrid stairs and filthy wet snow. Only Teddy sighed. He felt disappointed. "Fine heroes we turned out to be," he thought. "We wanted adventure, but the only adventure we've had is to get really dirty."

23 January

Being told off

Alice's mother was angry.
"Look at the state of your dolls and

your teddy bear Alice. They are covered in mud and soaking wet!"
Alice couldn't understand how it had happened.
"I didn't put them in the dolls' pram."
Her mother was annoyed with Alice.
"And telling lies now too Alice. Shame on you."
Rag Doll, Harlequin, Sally-Ann and Teddy regretted that they had stowed away under the dolls' pram because Alice was now in so much trouble.

24 January

In the washing machine

Alice's mother flung Rag Doll, Harlequin, Sally-Ann and Teddy into the washing machine, added some washing powder and turned on the machine. Whoosh, whoosh. It started to turn.
"Help! I'm getting giddy," squealed Harlequin.
"And I've got soap in my eyes!" cried Sally-Ann.
Rag Doll rather liked all the turning and spinning.
And it would get him nice and clean.
Teddy said nothing. He concentrated on holding his loose eye tightly with both his paws. It was hanging on by a thread.
Just imagine if the thread had broken in the washing machine.

25 January

Like new

Click ... the door of the washing machine opened. Alice's little fingers were searching for Rag Doll, Sally-Ann, Harlequin and Teddy. She took them out of the machine one at a time and put them up on top of a radiator.
They would dry nicely there.
"Mmm, nice and warm!" sighed the four friends contentedly. They smiled at each other.
They all looked so clean and smelled so fresh.
When Alice's mother had sewn up Teddy's ears and fixed his eye, they would all look like new.

26 January

Teddy is a baby!

Because Rag Doll, Harlequin, Sally-Ann and Teddy were so nice and clean, Alice was keen to play with them again. Teddy was really soft and fluffy. Alice decided to dress Teddy in Diane's clothes – a jumper and a hat. But what was Alice doing now? She was putting a nappy on Teddy.

Rag Doll and Harlequin couldn't stop laughing. "Ha ha ha! Teddy is a baby," they chuckled.

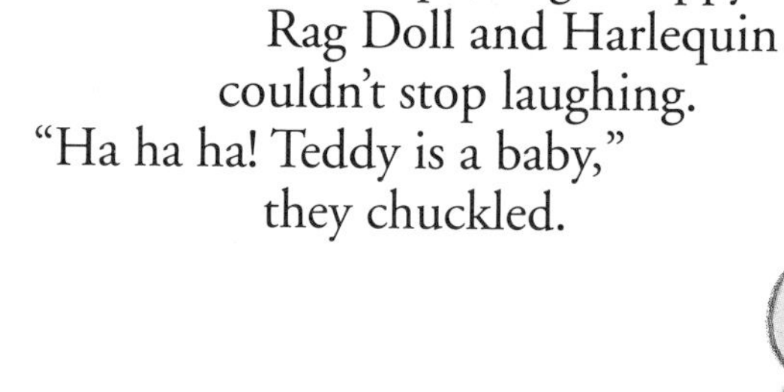

27 January

Floppy potty

Harlequin and Rag Doll soon regretted laughing at Teddy. Alice thought that her other toys needed to sit on the potty. She grabbed Harlequin first and put him on the potty. Rag Doll was next.

"I look so stupid," moaned Raggy. His long legs hung over the side of the potty, but his body was so limp, he couldn't sit upright.

"Here's a potty with legs and a head," giggled Teddy. "I'd much rather wear a nappy than look like you Raggy."

28 January

I want adventure

Alice loved to play games with her dolls. She dressed and undressed them, put them to bed and also bathed them. Sally-Ann was a bit bored with the same old routine.
"I'm an adventurous doll," she said. "I want to play dangerous games."
"Isn't she a clever clogs?" thought baby doll Diane. Rag Doll and Harlequin were thinking the same thing.
"I would like to see how well she copes with real danger," said Raggy.

29 January

A tiger

Sally-Ann was going to show them all how brave she was. She looked around the room. Suddenly the door opened. A large furry head with long whiskers and yellow eyes appeared. It was Kitty the cat. Kitty had quietly slipped upstairs.
She strolled around the room. Then she found the cupboard and with one swift jump she leapt in. She started to paw Sally-Ann.
"Help!" screamed Sally-Ann. "Go away! It's a tiger!"
Sally-Ann wasn't so brave after all, was she?

30 January **All to bed**

Alice had a new plan. When she went to bed, all her dolls and Teddy had to join her. Diane first, then Raggy, Harry and Sally-Ann. Alice put Teddy next to her because Teddy was lovely and soft. Then Alice crawled into bed. What a tight squeeze it was. "Help, I'm suffocating," gasped Sally-Ann. "Take that arm off my face," grumbled Harlequin. "You are making my foot itch," said Diane to Raggy. Teddy didn't say anything. He was really comfy lying on the pillow next to Alice.

31 January

Sleep well

With a huge smile on his face, Teddy snuggled under the sheets and closed his eyes.

With his deep bear's voice he mumbled softly and happily, "Good night, dearest Alice. Sleep well."

1 February

The Doll family

The Doll family lived in a stately dolls' house. It was a very old dolls' house with three storeys. On the ground floor was the kitchen and the living room. Father and Mother Doll's bedroom was on the first floor. Next to it was the bathroom. On the second floor were the children" bedrooms. And then right at the top, just beneath the roof, was the attic.
There were tiny pieces of furniture in all the rooms. There was a wonderful cooker in the kitchen and copper pans. In the living room there was a large open fire and big soft armchairs. There were even tiny flowers in a vase on the table. In the bedrooms there were little wooden beds with real blankets and pillows. There were pretty curtains in every room. Everyone in the Doll family was very happy with their lovely home. They all hoped they could stay there for a long time.

2 February **Pip**

"Oooaaah!" Little Pip Doll woke up.
He stretched. What was the time? Silence. He couldn't hear anything at all. Father and Mother must have been sleeping. Pip didn't feel sleepy. He decided to get up. Perhaps his sister Pam was awake too. Quietly he slipped out of his room. Knock, knock, he tapped on Pam's door. Silence.
"It must be too early to get up," mumbled Pip and he crept back to bed.

3 February **What time is it?**

Little Pip tossed and turned. He had been awake for ages and he was bored.
"Hmm," he moaned. "I wish I knew what time it is."
But there wasn't a real clock in the dolls' house. In the living room there was a pretend clock on the wall. The hands always pointed to quarter to three and Pip knew for certain it wasn't quarter to three. Then Pip had an idea. "There might be a big people's clock in the same room as our dolls' house?" He slipped out of bed and stuck his head out of the window. Take care Pip. Don't lean too far out of the window!

4 February **Too far**

Pip was hanging far too far out of the window. It was incredibly dangerous. He looked around. Where was the big people's clock? Perhaps in the corner? Pip leaned even further out of the window. And then ... tumbling, tumbling, Pip fell to the ground. Dear, oh dear, what a noise. The noise woke his father and mother. They ran to their window to see what had happened. They were very worried when they saw Pip on the ground. Fortunately Pip was a tough little doll. He was only a little dazed. Apart from that, he was fine. But when he told his father and mother what had happened, they sent him to bed to teach him a lesson.

5 February The sad bath

The bathroom in the stately dolls' house even had a bath. But no water ever came out of the gleaming tap. The bath was never filled with lovely hot and foaming water. The bath was rather disappointed.
"I long for water," it sighed. "Even just the odd drop. I stand here with nothing to do." The gleaming tap felt so sorry for the bath. So sorry in fact, that it started to cry. Drip ... drip ... drip. The tap's tears fell into the bath.
Now there was some water for the bath.

6 February The carpet-beater

Every evening mother Doll called to her children, "Time to wash. Pip! Pam!" How could dolls wash themselves? Because Pip and Pam never went outside, they never got really dirty. They only got dusty. That was why their mother took the carpet-beater and gently knocked the dust from their bodies. Pip and Pam hated it. "Ouch! Ow! Stop! Help!" Being bashed with a carpet-beater every evening wasn't much fun, they thought.

7 February **The paintbox**

"I don't want to be bashed with the carpet-beater tonight," muttered Little Pip angrily.
"Me neither," said his sister Pam. "I want a proper bath."
"Then," declared Pip, " we'll have to get really dirty. You can't get rid of real stains with a carpet-beater."
"How are we going to do that?"
Pip chuckled and pointed outside.
Pam's looked outside. Next to the dolls' house there was a paintbox.
"Do you mean ..."

8 February **Silly Pip, silly Pam**

Pip and Pam crept out of the dolls' house. They didn't want their parents to hear them because they had a really naughty plan. They wanted to make themselves look very dirty. There were lots of lovely colours in the paintbox – red, blue, green and yellow. But Pip and Pam didn't want pretty bright colours. They wanted duller colours like brown and black to make them look dirty. With a hop, Pip jumped right on top of the brown paint and with a skip Pam jumped on to the black. They rolled around and rubbed their bottoms in the paint. Silly Pip and silly Pam. It was watercolour. Without any water you couldn't paint anything – not even dirty patches!

9 February

No teeth

In Mother Doll's kitchen store,
You find no foods that are a bore.
Nothing but every kind of sweet,
Arranged in jars, in lines so neat.
Perhaps you want an aniseed ball,
You'll find that she has got it all.
Liquorice, toffees, bubble gum,
All things bad, but so much fun.
Are their mouths all full of fillings?
Do they brave the dentist's drillings?
They don't have to suffer grief,
For these dolls have got no teeth!

10 February

Shopping

Mother Doll was in the kitchen. She checked all the cupboards. She checked the drawers too.
"Oh dear, oh dear! We've used up all our food. We've got nothing in house." It was true. In the back of a cupboard there was a very small piece of cake, but that was all. She called Father Doll. "Father, it's time to go shopping again." Father Doll nodded his head. He knew what had to be done. That night, when it was dark, he would venture out.

11 February

Dangerous journey

In the middle of the night Father Doll was ready to depart. He was going shopping. Carrying a big rucksack, he climbed down to the floor. He had a long way to go. First he had to get out of the children's playroom, then cross the landing, go down the stairs and into the kitchen. He knew precisely where the food was kept. But for such a small doll this was a long journey. It was also very dangerous. Imagine if Father Doll were to fall down the stairs! Or perhaps he might encounter the cat on his expedition!
Mother Doll was so relieved when he returned several hours later with a rucksack full of food.

12 February

Can I go with you?

All the members of the Doll family were sitting at the table. Father Doll had just fetched new supplies from the big people's kitchen. What delicious things he had brought! Cinnamon biscuits, liquorice ... and a scrumptious cream puff. With his mouth full of whipped cream, Pip asked, "Can we go with you Dad, when you go shopping?" "No son, that's far too dangerous," said his father. "Oh Dad!" pleaded Pam. "We'll be careful." Pip and Pam wanted to go so much that eventually Father promised that they could go at some point in the future.

13 February

An adventure

Tonight was the night! Pip and Pam were going to join their father on his journey through the big people's house. The big people who lived there were away for a few days. It would be a bit safer for Pip and Pam. They still had to be wary of the cat though, because he was still at home,
"Are you nervous?" Pam asked her brother.
"Not at all," answered Pip, sounding brave.
But if you looked closely, you could see that his knees were knocking.

14 February Calm down!

"Are you ready?" Father asked Pip and Pam.
"Of course!" Pip and Pam couldn't wait to set off.
It was the first time they had ventured out into the world of the big people's house. They were in a hurry to get going.
"Calm down!" said their father sternly. "You must walk behind me, be very quiet and pay attention because the cat is somewhere in the house. If he sees us, he will think we are mice. And you know what a cat does with a mouse ..."

15 February The creak of a door

Pip and Pam followed their father through the big people's house. It was so exciting! They were so small compared with the gigantic furniture. Pip and Pam found it much more terrifying than they had imagined. They jumped at every sound – the ticking of a clock, the creak of a door. What was that? It seemed like they were being followed. Could it be the cat? Suddenly a newspaper fell off a table.
'Help!" screamed Pip and Pam and they ran as fast as possible back to the dolls' house. Father Doll chuckled to himself at his children who had so wanted to come on this adventure.

16 February

Reading lesson

The Doll children had to learn to read and do sums. There was no school for them though. That was why their parents taught them to read. They had borrowed one of the big people's books from a bookcase. It had been quite difficult to carry, because the book was so big. The book came from the bottom shelf so that they didn't have to climb down from one of the higher shelves with a book on their backs. The book was also less likely to be missed because the big people never looked at the bottom shelf.
"Look Pip and Pam," said their mother as she struggled to lift the pages. "Here are the letters of the alphabet and with these letters you can make any word you like." Pip and Pam looked at the big letters in the book with surprise.
"At least," laughed Pip mischievously, "we won't need glasses to read the letters. They are big enough for us!"

17 February Heavy work

"I wish reading wasn't such heavy work," sighed Pam Doll. Pip said nothing. He needed all his strength to turn the page. The book was at least four times as big as them.

"Phew!" Finally with a crash, he turned the page.

To read a sentence, Pip and Pam had to walk from left to right. Sometimes, as they were walking, they forgot the beginning of the sentence. Then they had to walk back to the beginning again. But the book was so exciting they quickly finished a page. It was Pam's go next to turn over the page.

18 February

The fun has just begun

If you are a tiny dolly,
Scarcely bigger than a thumb,
And still don't know your letters
Reading's not a lot of fun.

Since there are no books for dollies,
From the big ones you must learn.
With their large and heavy pages
That are so difficult to turn.

But when you know your alphabet,
The sentences soon come,
The pages turn more quickly
And the fun has just begun.

19 February **The attic**

At the top of the dolls' house, just beneath the slanting roof, was the attic. This was where Pip and Pam played. They had made a den in a corner beneath the sloping roof. Inside the den it was very dark, but Pip and Pam didn't mind.

It was their secret hiding place.

When Pip and Pam were in their den, they never shouted. In fact they always whispered. They called it their whispering den.

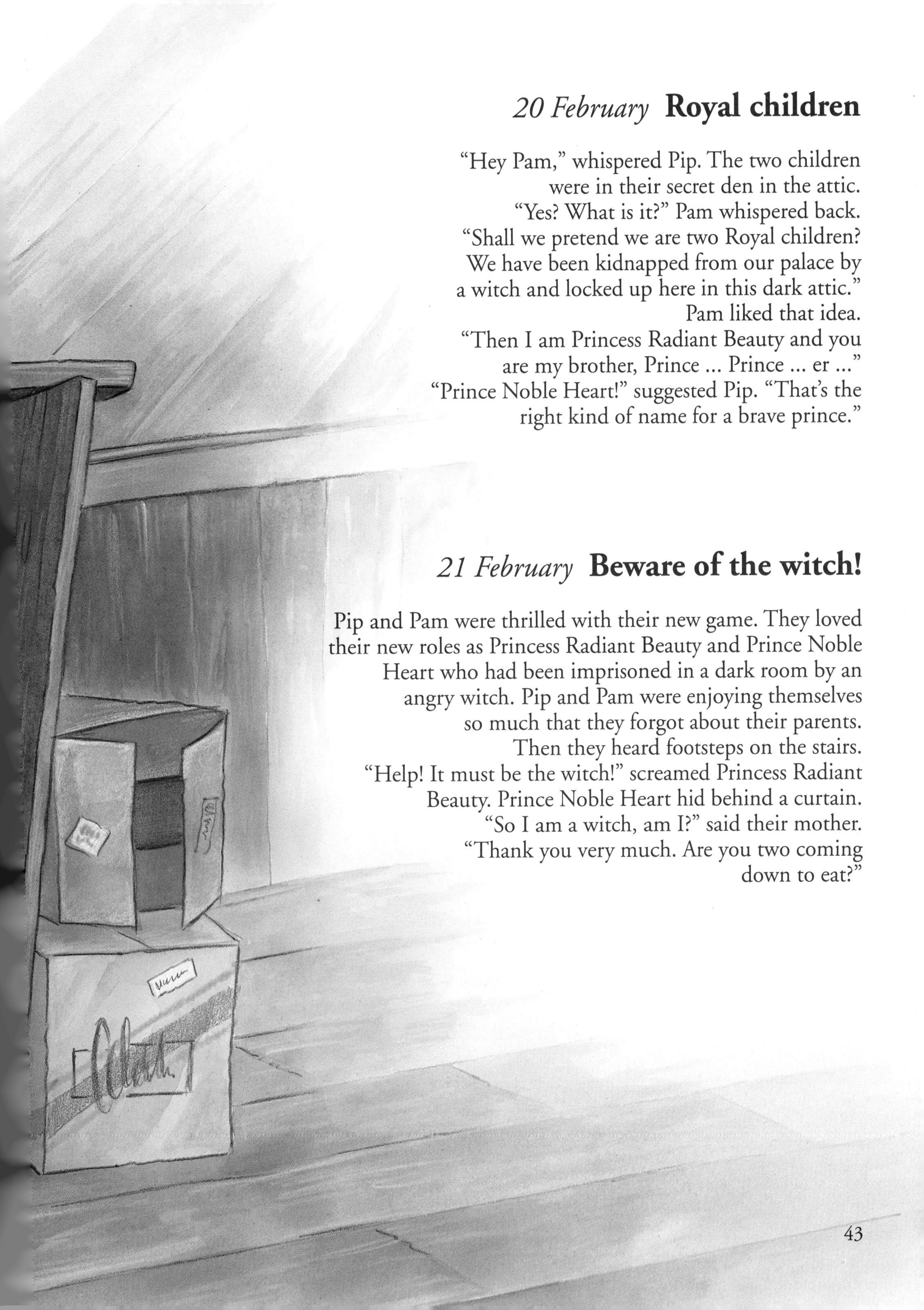

20 February Royal children

"Hey Pam," whispered Pip. The two children were in their secret den in the attic.
"Yes? What is it?" Pam whispered back.
"Shall we pretend we are two Royal children? We have been kidnapped from our palace by a witch and locked up here in this dark attic."
Pam liked that idea.
"Then I am Princess Radiant Beauty and you are my brother, Prince ... Prince ... er ..."
"Prince Noble Heart!" suggested Pip. "That's the right kind of name for a brave prince."

21 February Beware of the witch!

Pip and Pam were thrilled with their new game. They loved their new roles as Princess Radiant Beauty and Prince Noble Heart who had been imprisoned in a dark room by an angry witch. Pip and Pam were enjoying themselves so much that they forgot about their parents.
Then they heard footsteps on the stairs.
"Help! It must be the witch!" screamed Princess Radiant Beauty. Prince Noble Heart hid behind a curtain.
"So I am a witch, am I?" said their mother.
"Thank you very much. Are you two coming down to eat?"

22 February What's happening?

The Doll family enjoyed living in the big dolls' house. They had lived there for a long time. It had lots of space and, above all, it was very quiet. Always quiet? Well, it wasn't very quiet that day. What on earth was going on?
Huge hands emptied everything out of the house. The furniture was taken out piece by piece. When the dolls' house was empty, all the members of the Doll family were picked up.
"Help!" screamed Pam. She was put in a box with Pip and her mother and father.
The Doll family didn't know what was happening.

23 February Moving house?

The box was dark and frightening. They had been trapped there for a whole day. Mother and Father were worried.
"What's going on?" asked Pip and Pam. Their mother said quietly, "I really don't know. Perhaps we are moving house."
"Ooh!" cried Pip and Pam. "Are we moving too?"
"Perhaps," said Father. "But we could be going to the store room in the attic. We might have to stay in this box forever." Everyone was silent. What a horrible thought.

24 February

The button on the wall

Huddled in the dark box, the Doll family had almost given up hope. They thought they must have been banished to the attic forever. Then the box moved. And then ... bright light. The lid of the box had been taken off. One by one the dolls were put back in their old house. Mother and Father looked around. “Everything looks the same as before, but something has changed,” Mother said looking puzzled. The others looked around too. Suddenly little Pip called out, “There’s a button on the wall. That wasn’t here before.” He walked over to the button and pressed it. A bright light shone from the ceiling. “Oh, how wonderful!” they all cried. “We’ve got electricity.”

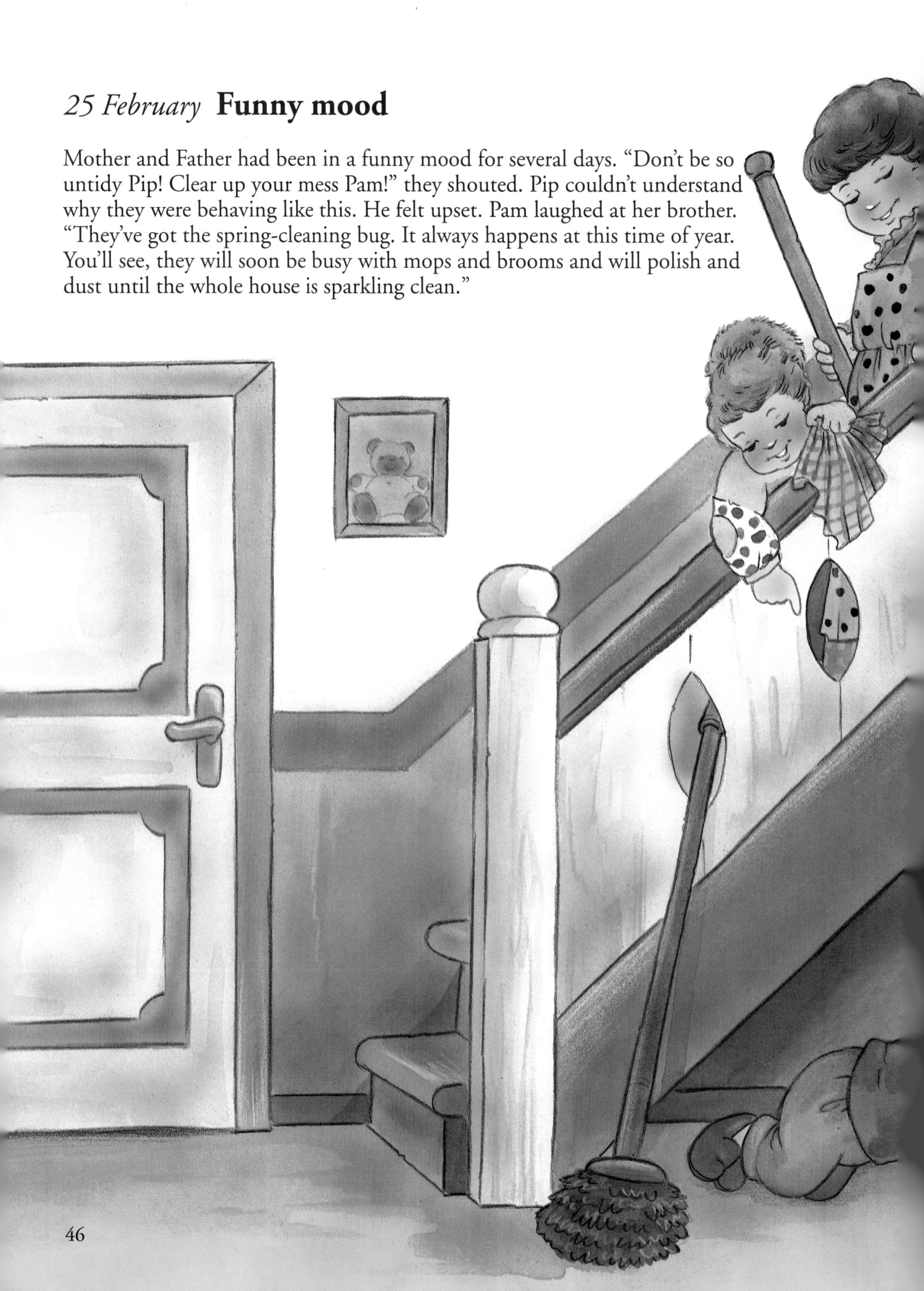

25 February **Funny mood**

Mother and Father had been in a funny mood for several days. "Don't be so untidy Pip! Clear up your mess Pam!" they shouted. Pip couldn't understand why they were behaving like this. He felt upset. Pam laughed at her brother. "They've got the spring-cleaning bug. It always happens at this time of year. You'll see, they will soon be busy with mops and brooms and will polish and dust until the whole house is sparkling clean."

26 February Duster, broom and mop

Armed with a large broom, their father was giving the whole house a good clean. Spring was on its way. Pip and Pam always had to help at this time of year. Pam got a duster and Pip got a mop.
"Pam, you must dust all the window sills and Pip you must clean all the cobwebs off the ceilings."
Father and Pam whistled and sung songs as they worked.
But Pip wasn't so cheerful.
"I'm bored with this now!" he grumbled.

27 February Lazy bones!

Mother, Father and Pam were busy. They had already dusted the front room and the kitchen. They decided to tackle the bedrooms next. When they walked up the stairs, Pam tripped over a handle.
"Hey, what's the mop doing here?" she said angrily.
"Pip was supposed to be using it."
"Where on earth has he got to?" asked Mother.
They all looked for Pip and eventually found him under the stairs. He was snoring!
"Well now, Pip! Having a little nap are you?"
Pam gave him a good shake. Pip woke up and spluttered, "Me? What? Oh no!"

28 February **A treat**

After they had cleaned from top to bottom, Father visited the big people's house. He came back an hour later. His rucksack was filled with lovely things.
"After all that hard work, we all deserve a treat," he laughed.
Keeping them all in suspense, he slowly opened the rucksack. He smiled.
"Daddy, don't keep us in suspense! What have you brought?" Pip and Pam shouted. He unpacked a ball and ten matches. The children were surprised.
They followed their father to the hall, where he set up all the matches in position. "Tonight we'll have a go at bowling," he laughed. "We'll see who can knock over the matches with the ball."
That evening the whole family had a great time bowling.
The children didn't want to stop!

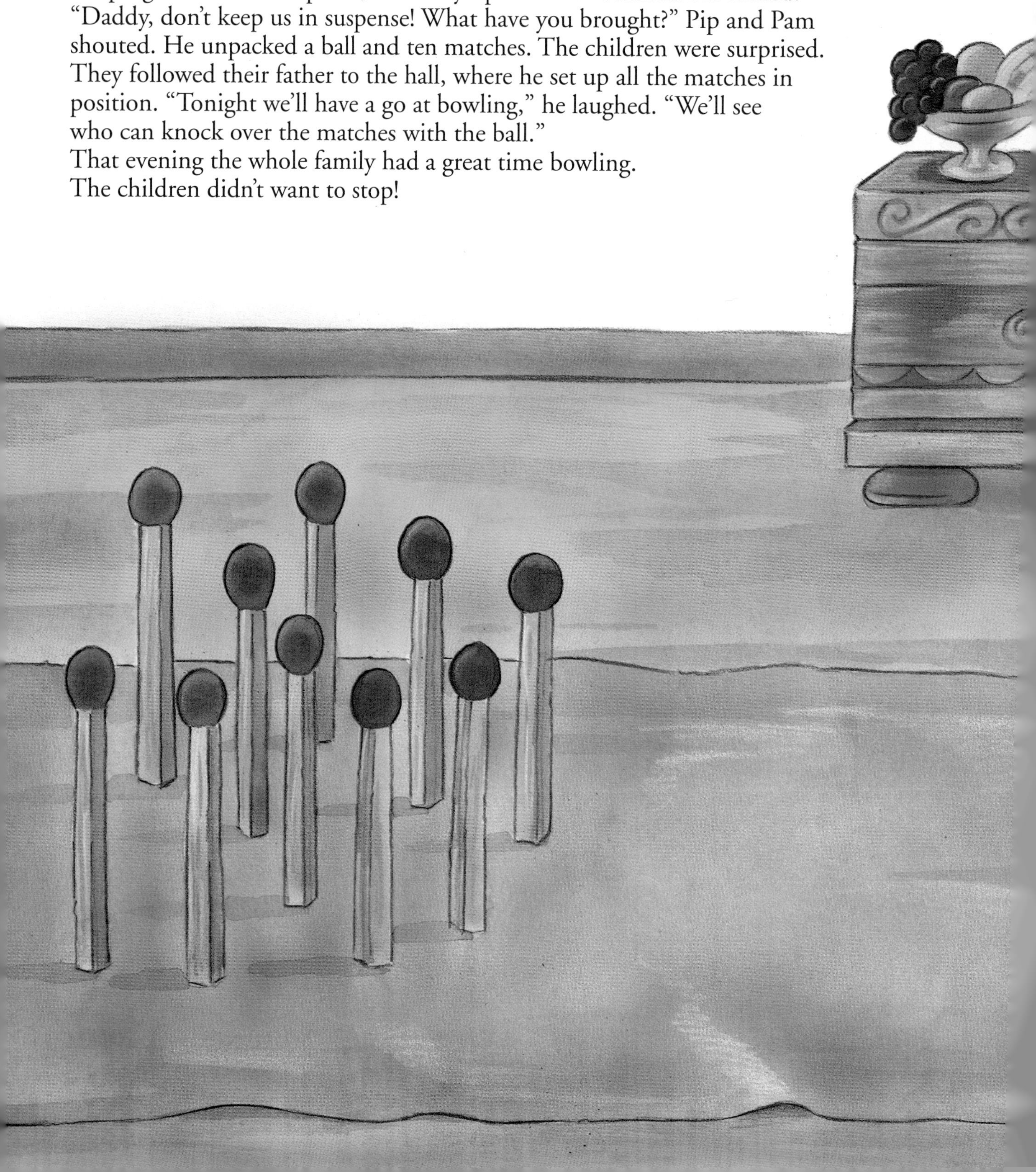

29 February **Bowling**

Keep you arm straight and aim the ball,
Watch it run way down the hall,
The pins should topple one by one,
Ten, nine, eight, until they've all gone.
It's my turn now, says Pip the young brother,
Watched with a smile by his father and mother,
He aims the ball slap-bang in the middle,
They all fall down, hey what a fiddle!
Pam's on next, she's longing for a go,
She decides to keep the ball
rolling low,
It slips and slides along
the floor,
Over they topple, five,
six, even more!

1 March **Freddie**

Up in Grandpa Dickinson's attic there was a wooden box. That box had not been opened for a very long time. In it were lots of toys. Grandpa Dickinson used to play with the toys when he was a boy. He was far too old to play with the toys these days. When he was young, his favourite toys were his tin soldiers. He remembered playing with them. One of his soldiers had only one arm. He called that soldier Freddie.

2 March **The wounded soldier**

Do you know how tin soldiers are made? First a hollow mould is made. The tin is melted and poured into the mould. The tin cools and sets. The tin soldier can only be removed from the mould when the tin has cooled. It's a little bit like making a jelly. Usually all the soldiers are perfect. But when Freddie was made, something went wrong. He was the last soldier in the mould and there wasn't enough tin left. So he only got one arm. When Grandpa played with his soldiers, Freddie was always the wounded soldier. That made Freddie quite different to the other soldiers.

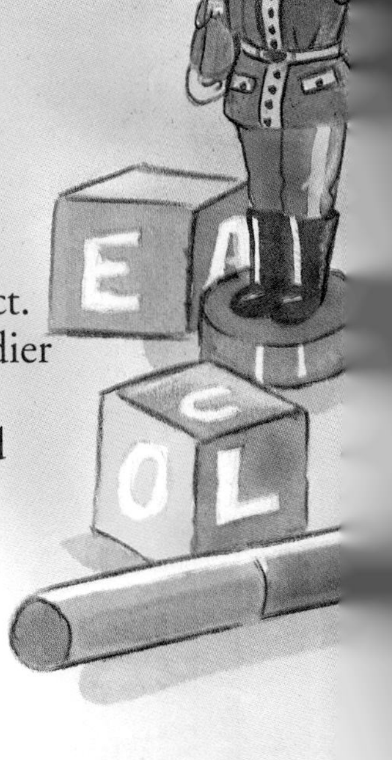

3 March **Freddie is bored**

Freddie was lying in the box with the other soldiers. He was bored. They were never taken out of their box nowadays. Freddie wasn't very keen on being a soldier really. He didn't really like games about war and fighting. But doing nothing year after year and lying in a box all day long was so much worse.

4 March **Teasing**

The other soldiers in the box always teased Freddie. It was hard for Freddie to hold a rifle with one arm.
"Hey Freddie, gives us a hand!" the soldiers yelled and laughed.
Freddie couldn't give anyone a hand of course.
"It's not my fault I wasn't made properly," Freddie muttered to himself. He had had enough. He wanted to get away, leave the others behind. So, he carefully made a hole in the top of the box with the end of his rifle. When the hole was big enough, he crawled through it.
"Goodbye guys! I'm off. I'm going to find a real friend!"

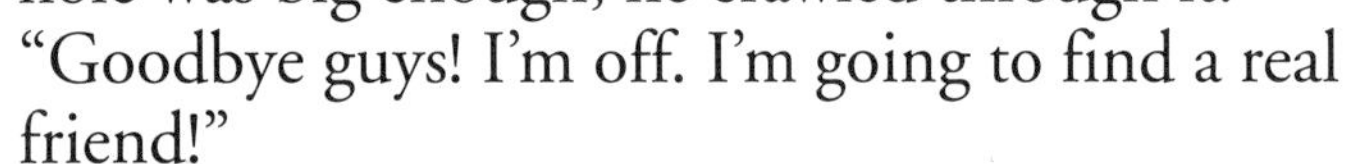

5 March

Rocking horse

Freddie stood in the middle of the attic. It was rather dark. The only light came from a small attic window. Between the boxes and crates there was an old rocking horse. Freddie walked over to it.

"Hello rocking horse. I'm Freddie. I've just escaped from that box and I'm looking for a friend."

The horse rocked gently backwards and forwards. He had been in the attic so long that his ears were full of dust. He didn't even hear Freddie's voice. Feeling rejected, Freddie turned away.

6 March

Where can I find a friend?

I am searching for a friend
To play with and to share,
Someone who is really nice
One who truly cares.

I have looked almost everywhere,
To see if I can find,
A dear, true loyal friend,
I can't get it off my mind.

7 March **Lonely**

Freddie searched through the whole attic for a friend, even in the smallest corners. He felt tears prick his eyes. If he wasn't such a brave soldier, he would have cried. He felt so lonely. Should he go back to the box with the other soldiers? Even though they teased him all the time, it was better than being alone.

8 March

Sybil the spider

Sybil the spider was sitting in her web in a corner of the attic. She heard someone sniffing. She looked down and saw Freddie. She slid down a long thread and stopped in front of Freddie. Freddie was a bit startled by the monster dangling in front of him. He ran off. Wait Freddie! Sybil only wanted to comfort you. Spiders know all about being lonely. Everyone is afraid of them.

9 March

Look out!

Freddie had been so scared by the sight of Sybil that he ran off without looking where he was heading. Look out Freddie! The stairs! But too late. Freddie tumbled over the stairs. Bumpity-bumpity-bump. He landed at the bottom of the stairs. What an adventure Freddie was having – first a monster spider and then a dangerous fall!

"And all because I want to find a friend," sighed Freddie.

10 March

Willie Mouse

"Good heavens, what a noise!" Freddie looked up to see who was speaking to him. He came face to face with a little grey mouse. "Don't you know that you must be quiet or the cat will find you and eat you up?" whispered the mouse.

"No, I don't understand. Who are you and what is a cat?" asked Freddie.

"One question at a time please! I am Willie Mouse and a cat is a horrible creature with huge yellow eyes, and teeth and claws as sharp as knives. It can run incredibly fast and it can splinter wood with one blow of its claw!"

Freddie thought that a cat sounded much worse than the horrible monster he had just seen. What a scary thought!

11 March

The monster

Little Willie, the house mouse
Tells ghastly tales of fright,
Of a horrid monster in a haunted house
That will carry you off by night.

In his vivid imagination
This monster was a cat,
With twelve legs and sharp claws,
One swipe and that would be that!

12 March **Danger**

Freddie the tin soldier and Willie the mouse were sitting at the bottom of the stairs. Freddie told Willie about the mean soldiers who had teased him and his adventures in the attic.

"Well, well! You've certainly been having an exciting time!" said Willie. He was quite jealous. He dreamt of having an adventure ... the search for the most delicious cheese, dangerous climbs to shelves full of delicious biscuits, and chasing off the giant monster cat with twelve legs. Suddenly his whiskers begin to twitch, his ears pricked up and his eyes opened wide.

He could smell danger!

"Come with me quickly," he whispered to Freddie. "The cat is coming!"

13 March The chase

Freddie followed Willie Mouse as fast as his little tin legs could carry him. According to Willie, the cat could appear at any moment. He preferred not to have anything to do with that terrible monster. But Willie was moving so fast!

"Hey Willie! Wait for me!" panted Freddie. Willie turned round and pointed in the direction of the stairs. Freddie looked back and saw a gigantic, terrifying black monster. The cat! It was heading straight for him. Aaarggh!

14 March Running for his life

Freddie was running for his life. He could feel the breath of the cat. Quick, he had to find a hole or gap that the cat couldn't get into. His eyes shot round the room. There was an open door! Freddie made a dash for it and pushed the door shut. It was quite amazing that a tiny tin soldier had closed such a big heavy door, but he had managed it.

"Phew! I'm safe for the moment!" panted Freddie. But what about Willie. Where had he got to?

"I've no sooner found a friend than I've lost him," moaned Freddie.

15 March **Locked in**

Freddie needed to get his breath back.
“Has that horrible cat gone away?”
he mumbled to himself. “I can’t hear anything. Shall I take a quick look?”
Freddie was horrified to discover that although he had got away from the cat, he had closed the door without thinking. How was he going to open it again? The door catch was far too high for a little tin soldier to reach.
Freddie was upset. All these dreadful experiences were getting on top of him.
He still felt like crying.

16 March **Who sleeps here?**

Freddie looked at the room. It wasn’t very big. There was a small bed with a pink bedspread and there were pretty flowery curtains at the windows. Freddie realised that this was a big person’s room.
He wondered who slept there. He decided to explore. He peeped in the cupboard, but it was completely empty. “How strange,” he muttered. “The person who sleeps here surely must have some clothes?”

17 March

New clothes

If I were a child,
The soldier reasons,
I'd have new clothes
For all the seasons.

In different colours
And made to measure,
Smart and casual
Would give me such pleasure.

I'd never wear
My uniform.
A nice new coat
Would keep me warm.

And on my feet
Instead of boots,
I'd wear nice trainers,
Oh what a hoot!

18 March

A visitor

Freddie was locked in. He couldn't get out of the bedroom. So, with great difficulty, he climbed on to the window sill. "At least I'll be able to look out of the window," he thought. He could see the garden. The wind was rustling through the grass and the flowers. On the other side of the garden was a neatly raked gravel drive. A car suddenly appeared. He could hear the gravel crunching as the car rolled over it. The car stopped and the door opened. A little girl stepped out. "Grandpa, where are you? I'm coming to stay with you for a few days." The little girl's father also got out of the car. Together they walked to the front door of Grandpa Dickinson's house and rung the bell.

19 March

Alison

Alison was Grandpa Dickinson's granddaughter. She was six years old. Alison's mummy had died two years ago and she still missed her so much. Whenever her daddy had to go away for a few days, she came to stay with her grandpa. He was very fond of Alison. He had arranged for one of his bedrooms to be decorated just for her. There was a lovely pink bedspread because pink was Alison's favourite colour. Her grandpa had another surprise for her. It was in a little box that he had hidden under the pillow.

20 March

Under the pillow

Freddie could hear the loud thuds as someone came up the stairs. They were heading his way, he was sure. It was Alison's room. Freddie was scared. He was sure he would be discovered and he would have to go back to the other soldiers in the attic. He slid from the window sill on to the bed. The door was opening. As quickly as he could, Freddie crawled under the pillow. Just in time!

21 March **The talking box**

It was dark and stuffy under the pillow.
"If these people don't leave soon, I'm going to suffocate," muttered Freddie.
"So will I!" said a small voice next to him. Freddie jumped and tried to see who was speaking to him. He couldn't see anything except for a small box. But boxes didn't talk surely?
"W-w-w-ho a-a-re you?" stuttered Freddie.
"I am Isabella and I am stuck in this horrible box," answered the voice.
Freddie thought it was such a pretty name that the person inside must be nice to talk to.
"Shall I try to get you out?" Freddie asked Isabella.
"Oh, yes please!"

22 March Isabella's escape

Freddie tore off the paper that covered the box with the end of his rifle. He was getting excited about meeting a new friend.

"How is it going?" asked Isabella from inside the box.

"I've got the wrapping paper off, but there is cardboard behind it and it is quite strong," explained Freddie. Fortunately tin soldiers don't give up easily, and after much prodding and tearing, Freddie had made a hole in the box. He helped Isabella to climb through it. It was very dark though and so he still hadn't been able to introduce himself to Isabella properly.

23 March

In love

Freddie slowly peeped out from under the pillow. No-one was around. The coast was clear.

"Come on Isabella, let's find a safer place to hide," he suggested.

Isabella appeared. She was so pretty that Freddie became shy and quiet. She had lovely red hair and bright blue eyes that were the same colour as the sky. Freddie had never seen anyone so beautiful before.

He knew he was in love.

24 March

Dirty mark

“Thank you so much,” Isabella said as she carefully stood up. “I don’t think I could have stayed in that dreadful box much longer.”
“A-a-a-a-t y-y-our service,” stuttered Freddie.
Isabella sat on the edge of the bed. She noticed her dress.
“Oh how awful, I’ve got a dirty mark on my dress!” she cried. “I’d better get rid of it.”
“Let me help you,” offered Freddie. He was pleased to be able to do something.

25 March

Helping Isabella

Freddie wanted to help Isabella, but he only had one arm and he was carrying his rifle with that. Slowly and carefully he took a handkerchief out of his pocket and put it on the end of his rifle. Then he pointed the end of his rifle at Isabella.
“I’m not very keen on pistols,” snapped Isabella.
“This isn’t a pistol, it’s a rifle,” explained Freddie. “The rifle is attached to my only arm. It may be a bit fiddly, but it’s the only way I can help you.”
“Well then, you’d better try,” sighed Isabella.

26 March **Accident**

Even though Freddie couldn't use his hands to rub off the mark, the end of his rifle and his handkerchief worked quite well. It took quite some time. Isabella was getting a bit impatient and started fidgeting. She turned round. That wasn't a good idea. The sharp point of Freddie's rifle ripped her lovely dress. "Clumsy oaf! Look what you've done!" screeched Isabella. She went bright red with anger and she stamped her little feet on the ground. Freddie wasn't very impressed. It had been an accident after all, and she was the one who had fidgeted and turned round too quickly.

27 March **Surprise for Alison**

Grandpa Dickinson was very fond of his granddaughter. That was why he had bought her a present. She would find it under the pillow when she went to bed. Grandpa chuckled to himself. He wanted her to open it now.
"What is it Grandpa?" Alison asked.
"Look under your pillow," answered her grandpa.
The little girl picked up the pillow. There was a box. It was very light. She quickly opened the box. There was nothing in it. Feeling a little disappointed, she handed the box to her grandpa. "But there isn't anything in there Grandpa?"
Grandpa couldn't understand it. Could the present have fallen out? He would have to look for the missing present.

28 March

Double present

When Alison saw her grandfather crawling around on his hands and knees, she realised that he hadn't played a trick on her. The box must have had something in it. She jumped off the bed to help him look.

"Perhaps the present has fallen under the bed," she said. Because Grandpa couldn't bend very well, Alison crawled under the bed.

"There is something here Grandpa," she shouted. She stretched out her hand and felt something hard. She managed to clasp her little fingers round it. She brought it out from under the bed. She was thrilled when she saw the two little dolls. A pretty girl doll and a tin soldier.

"Oh Grandpa, two presents! They are lovely," she said happily.

29 March

Thrilled to bits

Alison was asleep in her bed. Grandpa had also gone to bed, but he wasn't asleep. He was puzzled. He couldn't understand how the tin soldier had got under Alison's bed. He had forgotten that he had the soldier. It was so long since he played with all his old toys.
He had explained to Alison why Freddie only had one arm and how when he played with him, Freddie was always the wounded soldier.
Alison was really touched by the story.
"Oh Grandpa, that soldier is the nicest present I've ever had, because it is something you used to play with. I am thrilled to bits to have it."

30 March Wish

Freddie the tin soldier was on the window sill. The curtains were closed, but he could catch a glimpse of the dark night sky and the stars. Then suddenly a star shot across the sky. Do you know that you can make a wish if you see a shooting star?
Freddie sighed. "I don't need to make a wish. I'm so lucky. I never have to go back to that horrid attic and I have found the dearest friend I could possibly have," he said proudly.
"Do you mean me?" asked Isabella looking smug. Freddie didn't answer. Isabella was very pretty, but Alison was a much nicer person!

31 March

Shooting star

If you ever chance to see,
Against the dark night sky,
A falling, dazzling shooting star,
Don't let the chance pass by.

The moment will be only fleeting,
The times it happens are few,
Make a wish, think hard and long,
Your wish just might come true.

1 April

Little shop

Hidden away in the High Street was Doctor Spareparts' shop. It was a tiny shop, hidden between two big shops, so it was hard to see it. Yet all the children in the town knew Doctor Spareparts. He ran the dolls' hospital. He repaired all the broken dolls, teddy bears and other cuddly toys. He mended all the broken eyes, noses and ears so that they looked like new. Often he did some extra work on them too. He brushed the coats of cuddly toys until they shone. When the children collected their toys, they were thrilled with the results.

2 April

Doctor Spareparts

Doctor Spareparts was a kind man. He wore glasses with lenses as thick as jam jars. He had blue eyes and a wild grey beard. He wore a coat over his own clothes, but it wasn't a white coat, it was bright yellow. It had lots of pockets! He kept all sorts of things in his pockets – dolls' eyes, tubes of glue, brushes, his craft knife, his glasses, lots of things. Because he stuffed his pockets with so many things, he looked much bigger than he really was.

3 April Aunt Hetty

Doctor Spareparts was married to a nice friendly woman - Aunt Hetty. Aunt Hetty helped her husband as much as she could. She would make the most wonderful dresses, thick gardening trousers and brightly coloured blouses from bits of material. All the children were very fond of Aunt Hetty. When they visited the shop, Aunt Hetty always had a jar of sweets there.
"Go on poppet, take one," she said to the children who came in.

4 April Dingaling

"Dingaling, dingaling" tinkled the bell as the door opened and shut. Doctor Spareparts always knew when he had customers in his shop, which meant he could spend most of his time in his workshop behind the shop.
This was where he repaired the broken dolls and where he kept all his spare parts - dolls' arms and legs, eyes and heads. Sometimes a doll was so badly broken that it needed a new arm or a new leg. So Doctor Spareparts had a cupboard full of legs and arms in different sizes and colours. But whenever the front doorbell tinkled, Doctor Spareparts rushed straight through to the shop to see who was there.

5 April A dolly to repair

"Dingaling, dingaling..."
It's a really useful thing,
The bell fixed to the door,
No need to cross the floor.
The doctor is aware,
There's a dolly to repair.
Should his bell fail to ring,
He'd quickly fix the thing.
A broken arm needs prompt attention,
Any injury you care to mention.
Children should not have to wait,
He says, to learn the fate
Of their favourite doll or toy
A quick repair gives them joy.

6 April

Mischievous breeze

"Dingaling, dingaling!" Doctor Spareparts came out of his workshop to see his new customer. Puzzled, he peered through his thick glasses at the shop door. "How strange! There's no-one here. Perhaps I was dreaming," he muttered to himself. He was just about to pick up the scissors when the bell rung again. "Dingaling, dingaling!" But he still couldn't see anyone. "What's going on?" he said to himself. "Is someone playing a joke on me? I'll stand round the corner and see who is making fun of me." "Dingaling, dingaling!" went the bell. Can you guess who was playing a joke on the doctor? It was the wind. The door hadn't been shut properly and the wind kept pushing it open.

7 April **Winston**

Winston was four years' old. He had large brown eyes and dark curly hair. Tears trickled down his cheeks. Winston was very sad. His grandma had given him a cuddly toy monkey for his birthday. She had brought it all the way from Trinidad.
"You can't get one like this in England," he told everybody.
Winston loved his monkey. He took it to bed with him, on walks, and to nursery school. The other children were a little bit jealous of Winston's monkey and tried to grab hold of it. They had torn off his tail. That was why Winston was so upset.

8 April **Can he mend him?**

"Come on Winston!" said his mother "Stop crying!"
But Winston couldn't stop crying. "My pet monkey is broken. My best toy," he snivelled.
"Then we'll take him to Doctor Spareparts, the doll doctor. I'm sure he'll be able to repair your monkey."
Winston wasn't so sure.
"But my monkey came from Trinidad. He might have to go back there to be repaired."
"Oh, don't be silly Winston. Of course Doctor Spareparts will be able to mend him."
Winston felt a lot happier.

9 April **Warm jumper**

Holding mummy's hand Winston entered the shop. As soon as the bell rung, Doctor Spareparts stepped out of his workshop.

"Well, well young man, what a very special cuddly toy you have!" said the doctor and smiled.

"Yes, he comes all the way from Trinidad. That is a very hot country on the other side of the world," explained Winston proudly.

"Then I am sure your monkey must find it very cold here," said Doctor Spareparts. "I'll tell you what, while I make him better, my wife Hetty can knit him a nice warm jumper. I'm sure he'd like that."

Winston beamed.

"What a nice doctor he is," he thought.

10 April Being fair?

Doctor Spareparts was very busy. It seemed as if every toy in town was broken. He hardly had a minute to spare. "Calm down Spareparts," he mumbled to himself, "do one thing at a time."
There were ten dolls on his shelf all in need of repair. They all had tickets attached to their legs. On the ticket was the name of the toy's owner and when it had been brought to the shop. Doctor Spareparts could then mend all the toys in the right order. He liked to be fair. "Fair?" said the rag doll huffily. "If only the doctor knew how long I have been stuck in this cupboard without any stuffing!" But Doctor Spareparts didn't know what the dolls were thinking.

11 April Rag doll

Lisa was a rag doll. She was called Lanky Lisa because of her long arms and legs. Lisa hated being called that! "I get stuck with an awful nickname, Lanky Lisa," moaned Lisa.
There was a pretty doll sitting next to Lisa. The doll had dark pigtails and a bright yellow dress. "You're a bit floppy aren't you?" said the pretty doll. "Your legs just hang over the shelf." Lisa turned to her and answered angrily, "It's not my fault all my stuffing has fallen out. What can I do about it? I've been waiting for Doctor Spareparts to re-stuff me."

12 April **Lanky Lisa**

Lanky Lisa was upset,
She'd lost all of her stuffing,
She thought it would be kinder
If the other dolls said nothing.
Instead it's "My you're limp,
You're really flat in fact."
The other dolls really ought to learn
Some manners and some tact.
Lisa really was upset
That she looked so flat,
Without a total stranger
Saying things like that.
But Lisa, just remember this,
You are before her on the list!

13 April Careless

"Dear, oh dear," said Doctor Spareparts. "Not you again." On the other side of his counter stood a little girl with rosy cheeks, blonde hair and blue eyes. It was Emma. Emma was terribly careless. This was why she damaged her toys so often. She came at least once a month to Doctor Spareparts' shop to have something repaired. But it was less than a week since her last visit.

"Yes," said Emma cheerfully. "But this time it isn't for me. I have brought my brother's teddy bear. You can't imagine how careless he is!" Doctor Spareparts didn't reply. If Emma's brother took after her, he could easily imagine how careless he was!

14 April

A helping hand

Doctor Spareparts looked carefully at her brother's teddy bear. The damage wasn't too bad. One ear was a bit torn and the other was missing, but there wasn't any other damage. The bear was very grubby though. Emma stared at the doctor.
"What are you going to do, doctor?" she asked.
"The bear should go to Hetty," he replied. "She will wash him first before I repair him."
"Can I help her?" pleaded Emma. She really liked Aunt Hetty. Doctor Spareparts thought that it was probably a good idea for Emma to see how much work was involved in repairing damaged dolls and toys. Perhaps then she would take better care of hers.

15 April Working hard

Emma was in Aunt Hetty's laundry room. Aunt Hetty had run some warm water and added some washing powder and given Emma the job of washing the grubby teddy in the soapy water. After much scrubbing and rubbing, he looked a bit more presentable. Emma put the teddy on the draining board and got ready to go home.

"Hey ho! Where do you think you're going young lady?" quizzed Aunt Hetty. "I thought you wanted to help me? There are more dolls to be washed!"

Without a murmur, Emma got to work on the other dolls. She had never seen so many dirty toys. She really tried hard to get them all clean. Aunt Hetty was so impressed by her hard work, she gave her a big kiss and a bag of sweets.

16 April Is that the time?

Having finished her work, Emma had a look at Doctor Spareparts' workshop. There was a clock above his workbench. It was half-past four. "Goodness, is that the time? Mummy will be worried!" gasped Emma.

"Don't worry," laughed the doctor. "I telephoned your mother because I thought it might take a while."

The doctor thought of everything! But it was getting late, so she said goodbye.

"Thanks again for the sweets. I'd love to come again to help."

"Of course, any time Emma," said Doctor Spareparts.

17 April **Forgotten corner**

Most children loved their dolls and some of them cried when they had to leave their broken dolls with Doctor Spareparts. But they knew that he would make them better again. Yet there were other children who didn't seem to care about their dolls at all. It could be months before they collected them. There were even a few children who never bothered to collect their dolls. They were left in a corner of the workshop. This corner was known as the 'forgotten corner'. Most dolls were scared of the forgotten corner. They thought that once you went in, you never came out.

18 April **Dolly**

There was a little doll called Dolly in the forgotten corner. Dolly belonged to a two-year old boy who was learning to talk. He couldn't pronounce difficult names, so he simply called his doll Dolly. The little boy was so fond of his doll that he had cuddled it so hard he broke it. He had sucked her arms and legs too. He wouldn't let Dolly out of his sight though, so she never got washed. She was in a bad state. The boy's mother secretly brought the doll to Doctor Spareparts' shop. It might seem strange that this doll was sitting in the forgotten corner, but that was because the little boy had become very ill.

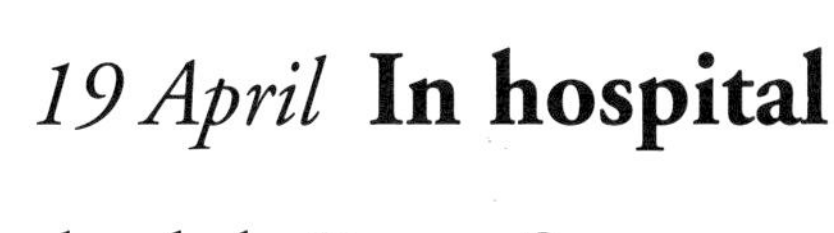

19 April In hospital

Emma had arrived to help Doctor Spareparts.
"Can you sweep the workshop floor Emma?" asked the doctor. "Then I can carry on working."
Emma cleaned every corner of the workshop, including the forgotten corner.
"Who does that little doll belong to?" she asked the doctor. "Which one?" he replied.
"Oh Dolly there belongs to a small boy called Sammy."
"Do you mean Sammy Kemble? The little boy who's in hospital?" Emma said.
"Is he?" gasped Doctor Spareparts. "I wondered why he hasn't been in to collect his doll. I know. We'll close the shop and take Dolly back to Sammy.
"What a lovely idea," said Emma.

20 April Hospital

It was visiting time at the hospital. Sammy Kemble was in bed. He had to get stronger before he could go home. The door opened and in walked a man and a little girl.
"Hello Sammy," said the man. "I'm Doctor Spareparts."
Sammy realised that yet another doctor had come to see him and he was a little frightened.
"I'm a doll doctor and I've brought you something."
Emma stepped forward with the package.
Sammy's little fingers opened the parcel. When he saw little Dolly, his eyes lit up.
He was so pleased to see her again.

21 April

A china doll

A beautiful doll of white china,
With the finest of lace for her dress,
And a face so delicate and gentle,
Should always be shown to impress.
Such a doll is too fragile and tender,
For the roughness of children at play.
She should always be put behind glass,
But never hidden away.
A doll that is made of china,
Of which there are only a few,
Ought not to fall from the dresser,
For she'll break both her arms in two.

22 April

A customer

A customer had come to the shop. Quite often Doctor Spareparts was visited by grown-ups who collected dolls. They loved to display their dolls. They collected mainly antique dolls. "Good morning Doctor Spareparts," she greeted him. "My valuable doll has fallen off the cabinet and both her arms are broken. I can't understand how it happened. I am always so careful." Doctor Spareparts nodded. He knew what had happened, but the customer just wouldn't believe him.

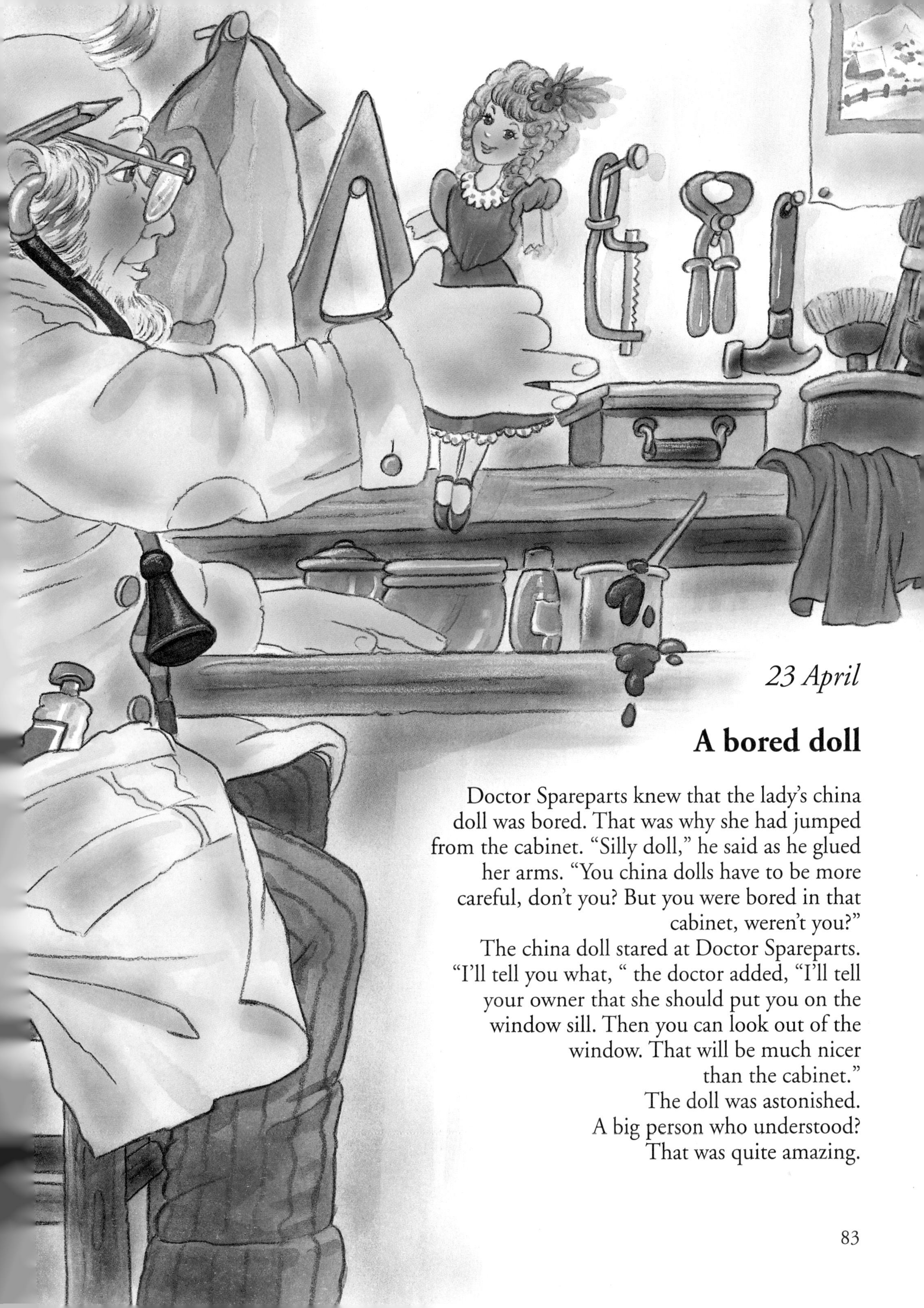

23 April

A bored doll

Doctor Spareparts knew that the lady's china doll was bored. That was why she had jumped from the cabinet. "Silly doll," he said as he glued her arms. "You china dolls have to be more careful, don't you? But you were bored in that cabinet, weren't you?"

The china doll stared at Doctor Spareparts.

"I'll tell you what, " the doctor added, "I'll tell your owner that she should put you on the window sill. Then you can look out of the window. That will be much nicer than the cabinet."

The doll was astonished.

A big person who understood?

That was quite amazing.

24 April

Bad eyesight

Doctor Spareparts had very thick glasses. He had bad eyesight. He couldn't see anything at a distance without his glasses, but his eyesight was better when objects were close to him. Sometimes when he had to join two seams or fit a very small eye, he could do it better without his glasses. Then he would put his spectacles in one of the pockets of his yellow coat. They were safe there and there was no danger of him sitting on them. He had broken them like that before. And Doctor Spareparts really couldn't do without them.

25 April

Where are my spectacles?

Doctor Spareparts shuffled round his workshop. He picked up dolls, opened drawers and looked under the table. Doctor Spareparts had lost his spectacles. What had he done with them? "I really need my glasses to look for them!" he muttered to himself. Oh dear, what a bother it was.
"Now think carefully Spareparts," he said.
"I was busy with Clara's little doll. I still had them then. I had almost finished the doll. I just had to fit an elastic band. I can do that best without glasses, so I took them off. My glasses must be next to Clara's doll!"
He went over to the doll, but they weren't there.

26 April **Clever Andrew**

"Dingaling, dingaling" tinkled the bell.
"Good afternoon," said a young boy. It was Andrew.
He had come to collect a cuddly toy.
Doctor Spareparts leant over the counter to see
who was in the shop.
He recognised Andrew.
"Hello Andrew," he bellowed. "This silly old man has
lost his glasses. That's why I had to lean over to see
who you are." Andrew laughed.
"Your glasses are on top of your
head Doctor Spareparts."
The spectacles had been sitting on
his forehead the whole time!

27 April Having a rest

Doctor Spareparts' workshop looked just like a hospital. Broken dolls were lying around, some with an eye missing or a crack in their tummy or a hole in their head. Yet it wasn't a sad place because dolls don't feel any pain. Of course they missed their owners a little, but they did get the chance to have a nice rest lazing on the shelf. When children played with them every day, it was nice to have a break.
"It feels like I'm on holiday," sighed one doll with long plaits. "Yes," agreed the doll sitting next to her. "I love having a rest." She yawned and closed her eyes.

28 April Let's have some fun!

"Hello sleepy-heads! Wake up!" shouted a doll with red curly hair. She had spent a week in the workshop. In that week she had slept quite enough.
"Don't you get bored?" she asked the other dolls.
"I find it a bit quiet," admitted a baby doll.
"You're right," said Lisa the rag doll.
"It's deadly dull here!"
"I miss having children around. The days go by so fast," said Sally-Ann.
"When Doctor Spareparts goes to bed, let's have some fun," suggested the red-headed doll.
"Great idea," agreed the other dolls.
"What shall we do?"

29 April **Conga**

When Doctor Spareparts turned out the light that evening in his workshop, the dolls began to shuffle about. They were looking forward to having some fun. The baby doll suggested that they did the conga through the workshop. "You know the conga, when we all dance along in a line one behind the other," she explained.

"But my leg is broken," cried one of the dolls.

"Then I will carry you on my shoulders," offered Harlequin.

They all lined up. "Let's go!" yelled Harlequin. They danced and sang songs for about an hour. What a night they had. They were tired out and ready for a sleep.

30 April **Let's dance!**

Put your best foot forward
And skip along the floor,
It's time to dance the conga
Until your feet are sore.

The arms go round the waist,
Until you have a line
Of happy dancing people,
The fun is really fine.

Dolly, Harlequin and Lisa,
And the baby doll too
Follow the dance around the room,
If only it were you!

1 May

Stuck in a box

Mandy stood on a shelf in a toy shop. She looked out of her box. Her eyes were so big and blue that it made her look as if she had been surprised by something. She had been. She was amazed by all the lovely things lying next to her on the shelf. There were boxes with pretty dresses inside.
"Oh, I wish I could get out of this box," she sighed.
"Then I could try on some new clothes."
She knew which dress she would try first. At the far end of the shelf, there was a wonderful party dress. It was turquoise with glittery bits on it.
"It would be such a nice change to try it on," sighed Mandy.

2 May

A change is good for me

"I'd love to try that dress,"
Said Mandy, feeling a mess.
"That dress is just so pretty,
It would be such a pity,
Not to try it on
When the others have all gone.
I'm tired of this old box,
And my pink dress and these socks,
A change is good for me
Quite different I would be."

3 May **Sold**

It was very busy in the toy shop. People were taking things off the shelves to have a good look at them.
"Help! What's happening?" shrieked Mandy.
She was being shaken around. Someone had picked up her box and she felt a bit dizzy. Then she felt a thud. Then she couldn't see anything. Darkness. The box had been wrapped up. Bang, bang, bang. Bounce, bounce, bounce. The carrier bag she was in was being knocked against someone's leg. "What on earth is happening?" Mandy panicked. Mandy had been sold.

4 May **Aunt Pauline**

Katy had a really nice aunt - Aunt Pauline. Unfortunately Katy didn't see her very often because she lived a long way away. Once a year Aunt Pauline came to stay with them. Because Aunt Pauline had no children of her own, she spoilt Katy. This time she had brought a large box with her. She had a surprise present for Katy. When Katy opened the box she found a beautiful doll and lots of lovely dolls' clothes. Aunt Pauline had made the clothes herself.
"Thank you so much!" shrieked Katy with delight and gave her aunt a great big kiss. She wanted to get everything out of the box. She looked at her new doll. She had lovely hair and big blue eyes. On the box it said her name was Mandy.
"Mandy?" sighed Katy. "That's just the right name for her."

5 May Clothes

Aunt Pauline had made a collection of about twenty dresses, trousers and shirts for Mandy because she remembered how much she had enjoyed changing her doll's clothes as a child. Katy decided to change Mandy's clothes. She chose a yellow top and a red skirt. Mandy wasn't too happy. "Yuck!" she moaned. "Yellow and red! I look like a parrot!"

6 May Tie it up!

Do I need to brush my hair?
It's really full of knots,
Perhaps a cut, if I dare,
Or tie it up, why not?

7 May The toy cupboard

When Katy wasn't playing with Mandy, she always put her away. Katy looked after Mandy. She had never had such a lovely doll before. She folded up Mandy's clothes and put them in the toy cupboard. Katy's other toys were also in the cupboard. On the top shelf were games and puzzles. Underneath there was a shelf filled with books and below that was the shelf Mandy shared with the other dolls. The other dolls were quite different to Mandy. They were softer, bigger and cuddlier, because Katy had got them when she was much younger. Mandy turned up her nose at the old dolls.
"What an ugly bunch," she said and turned to show them her own pretty face.

8 May The old dolls

Katy's old dolls stared. They had never seen such a beautiful doll. At first Mandy didn't want to speak to the other dolls, but she enjoyed being admired.
"What's your name?" one of the dolls asked.
"Mandy." "What a nice name," replied the doll.
"Much nicer than Mary. I don't like Mary." "That is so old-fashioned," sneered Mandy. "Who on earth is called Mary nowadays?"
"What's wrong with the name Mary?" whispered a little voice. It was Katy's old teddy bear, who had been listening to the dolls. "What you are called is not important," said Teddy. "How you look isn't important either. It's how nice you are to other people that counts."

9 May

Don't touch

"Would you like to see my clothes?" Mandy asked the other dolls.
"Have you got other clothes?" They were surprised.
"Oh yes, I have dresses, skirts, trousers and jumpers," she said with pride.
The doll called Mary couldn't believe it. Mary owned only the dress she was wearing. All the dolls looked inside Mandy's box.
"How lovely!" they all exclaimed as she pulled a dress from the box.
"Hey, don't touch!" shouted Mandy angrily. "You can look, but that's all."
"But, why can't we touch them?" Mary asked.
"You ... you ..." stammered Mandy, "... might make them dirty."
Teddy was really annoyed.
"Oh, so we are allowed to admire them, but not to share them. I don't think that's very nice at all."

10 May What shall we do?

It was raining outside. Katy didn't mind. She enjoyed playing with Mandy. But after she had changed Mandy's clothes a few times, she began to get bored. "What shall we do?" she asked her doll. "Let's go shopping and you could buy me some lovely new clothes," Mandy thought. But Katy, of course, couldn't understand what Mandy wanted. Katy chatted away to Mandy. "What? You would like a new home? What a great idea!"
Katy got excited. She started to gather bits and bobs - handkerchiefs, an old cushion, some wooden bricks and a pocket mirror.

11 May A new home

Katy made a home for Mandy under the table. She made the bedroom first. She laid the old cushion in a corner and spread a handkerchief over it. That was Mandy's sheet. "So Mandy, it's time for bed, while I build the rest of your house," Katy said to Mandy. She laid Mandy on the cushion and draped the handkerchief over her. Then she made a dining table and two stools with the wooden bricks. Then Katy got started on the living room. But she was stuck for a moment. How was she going to make the living room? She took three pairs of socks out of her bedroom drawer. She folded the socks to make the chairs – a red one, a white one and a blue one. Then she took a wooden block and a piece of card to make another table. There! Mandy's home was finished.

12 May **A mirror**

Katy was proud of the home she had made for her doll. She had even made a dressing-table in the bedroom. She had put her mother's pocket mirror on top of a box. Mandy was very happy when she saw the mirror on the dressing-table. "A mirror! How interesting!" she thought

13 May **It's gone!**

"Katy, have you seen my mirror?" It was Katy's mother. "Oh dear," Katy thought. She had taken her mummy's mirror. She picked it up and took it downstairs to her mother. Luckily her mother didn't mind too much. Mandy, though, was very upset when she found the mirror had gone. "Where has that mirror gone? I didn't even get the chance to look in it to see how pretty I am!" Poor old Mandy was on the verge of tears.

14 May

Lots of beads

Katy was stringing tiny beads on to a thread. She was making Mandy a necklace. Because Mandy had a small, thin neck, the necklace couldn't be too long or too heavy. Katy was concentrating hard. She fed the thread through a red bead, then a green one, and then a white one. "Phew! This is slow work," Katy sighed. "I've been doing this for ages and look how few beads I've strung." She stopped for a drink of lemonade. Then she started threading again – a red bead, a green one, white, red, green, white. The necklace was getting longer. "It looks long enough now," Katy decided. She tied a knot in the thread and cut off the end. Then she joined one end of the necklace to the other. The necklace was ready. What would it look like on Mandy?

15 May The necklace

Carefully, Katy tried to hang the necklace round Mandy's neck. Oh no! It was too small. It wouldn't fit over Mandy's head. Katy was upset. She really didn't feel like starting all over again. What could she do? It would be a shame to throw away the necklace because it was quite pretty. Katy had an idea. She grabbed Mandy and pulled her head off! "That should do it," she thought. She put the necklace round Mandy's neck and put her head back on. It was a little bit fiddly, but she managed it. There was a frightened look in Mandy's eyes, but that wasn't surprising since her head had just been pulled off her body!

16 May Not a pretty sight

It is not a pretty sight,
And some might say a fright,
To see a doll without its head,
Though very fortunately not dead.
But the beads I carefully strung,
Using fingers and my tongue,
Did not fit over her head,
So I did something
else instead.
I pulled her head
off quick,
I was worried I'd
make her sick.
But luckily she felt no pain,
And the beads looked
perfect, all the same!

17 May **Mark**

Katy had a little brother. He was two years younger than her and his name was Mark. She couldn't really play with Mark very much as he was too young. She could play games like hide-and-seek and tag, but she couldn't play with her dolls with Mark.
He couldn't really dress the dolls with his tiny fingers.
"Can I play with you?" Mark asked his sister. "Okay Mark.
Shall we play with the cars. I'd like to do that," said Katy.
She couldn't play with dolls all the time; it got too boring.

18 May **No peace**

Mandy was terrified of Katy's little brother. Sometimes, Mark liked to play with the dolls too and once he changed Mandy's dress. Mandy trembled when she remembered how Mark had pulled her about so much that the dress had ripped. No, Mandy was afraid of little brothers. "Let Mark play with Teddy. Teddy can take a few knocks," she muttered to herself.
"Or let him play with the bricks or cars.
Then he will leave me alone." Unfortunately for Mandy, Mark didn't want to play with Teddy or with the bricks. He wanted to play with his big red fire engine. So did Katy.

19 May **The fire engine**

"What should we do?" Katy asked Mark.
"Well," said Mark, "we'll make a house for Mandy and then we'll pretend the house is on fire. Then the fire brigade will come and put the fire out."
"Brilliant!" cried Katy and she started to build the house. When the house was ready, she got Mandy and put her inside.
"Help! Help!" screamed Katy.
"Dahdah, dahdah ...!" Mark was making the sound of a fire engine. He was going to save Mandy.
He stopped with a screech of brakes outside Mandy's house. He grabbed the hose, aimed it ... and squirted water all over Mandy. Mark's fire engine really could squirt water!
Mandy was furious. "That dreadful boy, I might have guessed he'd do something like this!"

20 May

Radio

"Mummy, can I have the radio?" Katy asked her mother.
"The radio? Which radio?" Her mother was busy and wasn't listening to Katy properly.
"The radio from the kitchen," Katy explained.
"The old one that you never turn on any more.
I will put it away afterwards."
Mother agreed. "Provided you look after it Katy.
It may be old, but there is no need to break it."
"No, I promise I'll look after it," Katy said.
What was Katy going to do with a radio?

21 May

To the disco

Back in her room, Katy shut the door. She was planning to play 'going to the disco' with Mandy.
And she needed music to play that game. She dressed Mandy in her best party clothes.
Mandy was delighted when Katy put on a pair of bright pink trousers and a pink top.
Katy looked a bit concerned.
"Perhaps I should try some other clothes?" she thought.
But Katy was impatient.
She wanted to turn on the music.

22 May **A change of clothes**

When Katy switched on the radio, she only heard talking. She turned one of the knobs. The radio hissed and crackled. Eventually she found some music. She liked it, but it wasn't really music that Mandy could dance to.
"What shall I do now?" Katy sighed.
"I think I'll have to change your clothes after all Mandy. I'll find some that go with this music." Mandy was rather pleased with her pink dress, but when she saw the new outfit she was even happier. It was a short skirt, long boots and a waistcoat. "Now, let's dance!" thought Mandy.

23 May

I'm bored

Katy was bored. Her little brother was playing with a friend. It was raining outside again and her best friend was ill. Have you ever noticed that when you are bored, even your favourite games seem boring too? Usually Katy was happy to play with Mandy. But she just couldn't be bothered. She took the doll out of the cupboard and slowly walked downstairs. Her mother was reading.
"I'm bored," sighed Katy. "Can you think of something I could do?"
Katy's mother thought for a moment and then suggested that Katy could make some clothes for her doll. Katy's eyes lit up.
What a brilliant idea!

24 May

Sewing

Katy looked first for some material. There was a big bag of old clothes and bits of material under the stairs. Katy found lots of pieces she liked, but eventually chose a blue piece and a red piece.
Mother told Katy what she should do. She had to cut out the pieces of the dress, remembering to measure them and to leave holes for her arms and head.
Her mother helped her with the cutting. Then she got a needle and thread and she started to sew the pieces together. She worked all morning. At last, it was time for Mandy to try on the dress.

25 May

It fits!

Katy pulled the dress very carefully over Mandy's head and put her arms into the sleeves. She fastened up the dress. Well, it fitted Mandy perfectly. Katy felt very proud that she had finished it.

"You've made a really good job of that Katy!" her mother said and smiled.

As a finishing touch her mother found a long piece of satin ribbon.

"Look, you can tie this around the dress Katy." Even Mandy was pleased with her new dress.

26 May

A big argument

Katy shouted angrily at Mark. “No, you can’t play with me.
You break everything!”
Mark shouted back. “No I don’t. I don’t break everything!
It’s not true!”
“Yes it is!”
“It’s not!”
“ ’tis!”
“ ’snot!”
Oh dear! Katy and Mark were having a big argument.
They didn’t really know why, it’s just something that sisters and brothers do.
Katy ran to her room and slammed the door. That meant it was out of bounds for Mark. So he stood outside on the landing and yelled through Katy’s door. She was a lying witch, and a really horrible, nasty sister. Katy yelled back.

27 May **Scissors**

Mark was upset and went downstairs. Katy was really stupid, he thought. Grumbling and mumbling to himself, he walked into the living room. Katy's doll Mandy was lying on the floor. Katy had forgotten to take her upstairs. Normally she was very careful with Mandy. Mark seized his chance and grabbed Mandy. He would show Katy. She wouldn't be happy when he had finished with her doll. She had stupid long hair he thought. It just got in the way when you played with her. Then Mark saw the scissors ...

28 May **Forgiven**

"Help!" Mandy screamed in terror. She knew that Mark wasn't to be trusted. He was looking a bit mean with those scissors. She knew that he wanted to cut off her lovely long hair! "Help!" she cried again. "Mark!" shouted their mother. She had seen her son grab the scissors and she stopped him just in time. "Stop that! She doesn't belong to you!" His mother told him to take back Mandy to Katy. When she saw Mark standing there with her doll, Katy forgave him. She knew he was trying to say sorry. Mandy was especially relieved that she still had her lovely long hair.

29 May

Fibber

Whenever Mandy had an adventure, she told the other dolls in the toy cupboard. Usually she made everything sound much more exciting than it actually was. The other dolls didn't realise this. Her stories were so exciting. Teddy knew though. He sat quietly in his corner on the shelf and listened to Mandy. "What a fibber," he thought to himself. "This can't be true." But he didn't say anything. Mandy knew that Teddy didn't believe her. She thought he was an old grouch. But, despite that, she would still have liked to be his friend. He looked so big and soft. Someone to snuggle up to and to tell all your secrets to.

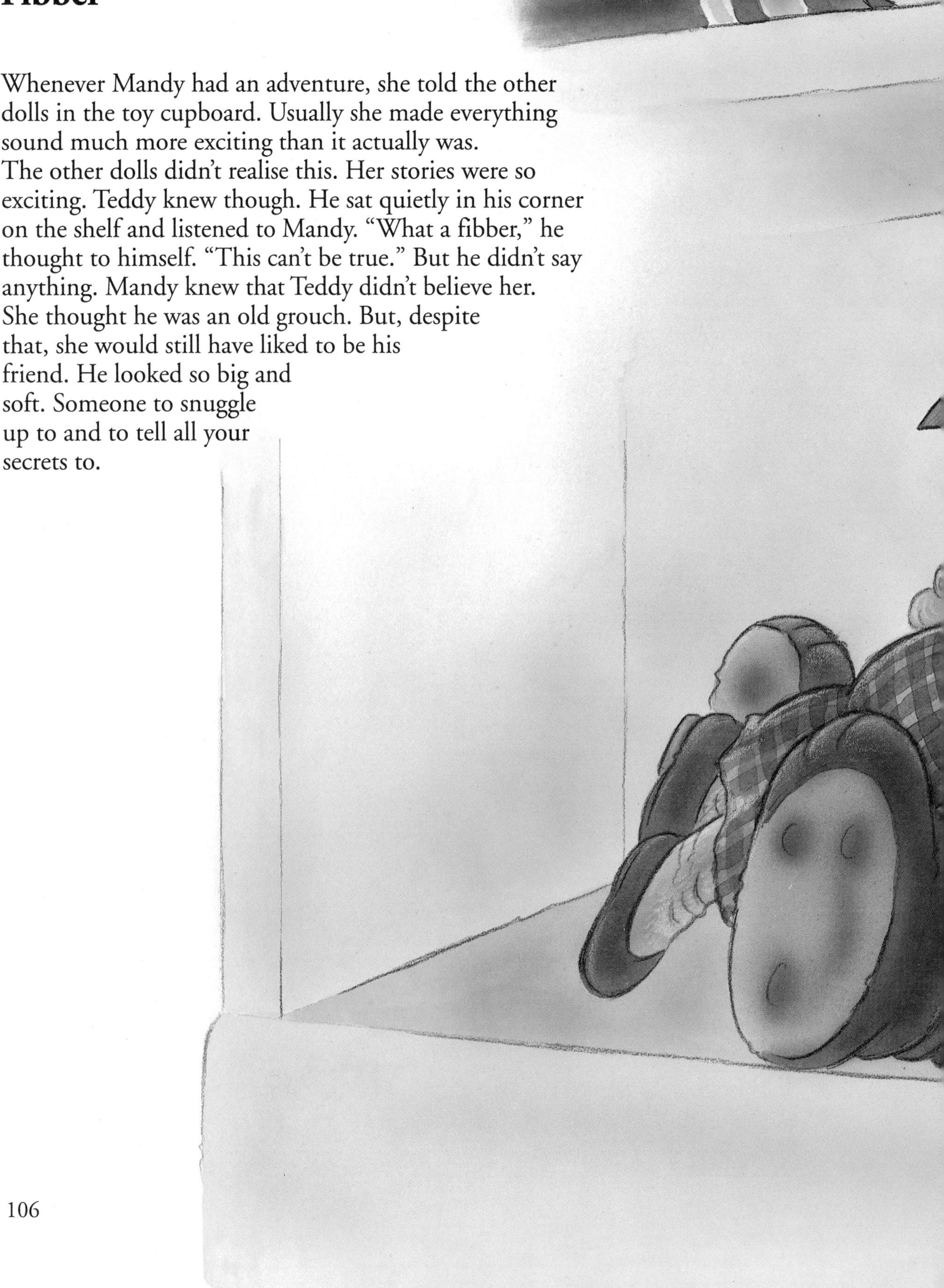

30 May

Come here then

Teddy sensed that Mandy had been staring at him for several days now. But whenever he looked in her direction, she looked away. "Come on Mandy!" he said to her. "What's the matter? You can tell me." Teddy's voice was so warm and friendly that Mandy decided to tell him.

"I would like to sit on your lap," she whispered.

"Are you going to boast about your pretty dresses and your exciting adventures then?" Teddy asked.

"No," promised Mandy.

"And you won't boast about your pretty face?" Teddy asked.

"No, definitely not," Mandy promised.

"Come here then," laughed Teddy and she sat on his lap.

31 May

Sitting on your lap

Sitting on your lap,
I feel so content.
You are so soft and big.
I can tell you everything.
Sitting on your lap
I feel so safe
And soon forget
My greatest cares.

1 June The nursery school

In the middle of the square was the nursery school. It had huge windows that let in lots of light. The children had painted pretty pictures on the windows. There was a cat and a dog, a clown and an elephant. A ray of sunshine shone through between the dog and the clown. It crept over the tables and underneath the chairs. Crossing the teacher's desk, it dived into the corner. The ray of sunshine looked around. The corner was full of dolls. There were ten of them! The ray of sunlight had never heard about a dolls' corner.

2 June The doll's corner

Ten dolls lived in the dolls' corner at the nursery school. There were five baby dolls, a rag doll called Sophie, a little doll with brown hair called Carla, and another doll with blonde plaits known as Greta. Then there was a wooden doll called Charlie and finally a clown who was just called Clown. All the baby dolls were called Baby.

3 June Five babies

The five baby dolls were sitting side by side in the dolls' corner. They all looked different, even though they were all called Baby. They had decided to give themselves a number. So they were called Baby One, Baby Two, Baby Three, Baby Four and Baby Five.

4 June A fight

The school bell had rung and the infants had gone home. The dolls could now get some peace. They liked to sit and chat to each other about the day. "Phew!" said Sophie. "It isn't always fun being a doll. Today Marianne and Carl had a row. They both wanted to play with me. Marianne grabbed one arm and Carl the other. They pulled so hard that they almost pulled me apart. It was lucky that Miss Jenkins stepped in before they tore me apart!"

5 June

Poor doll

Marianne was mad at Carl,
And he was mad at her,
If they both kept on tugging at Sophie,
She was probably going to tear.

The dolly was pulled from end to end,
To tear her apart, what a fate,
But thankfully teacher saved her,
She was not a moment too late.

6 June

Little Carl

All the dolls knew that Carl was trouble. He was always getting into mischief. They thought they should teach him a lesson. But what could they do? They sat down and thought about it. Then the clown had an idea. He rounded up everyone and told them his plan.

7 June Teach him a lesson

Carl came into the nursery. As soon as he picked up a doll something went wrong. One doll's arm fell off. Another doll's leg did the same. A baby doll's tummy wouldn't stop peep-peeping. Carl had to keep going up to the teacher to ask her to mend them. When he went up to her again, she told him that if he wasn't able to take care of the dolls, then he wouldn't be able to play with them. The dolls winked at each other. They had won. They had made their arms and legs loose. Dolls can be pretty clever, you know!

8 June Where is Greta?

"Where is Greta?" asked Baby Two.
All the dolls except Greta were in the dolls' corner.
"Maybe the infants forgot to put her away," suggested Carla.
"Then we must go and have a look," said Baby Five. Clown and Baby Four looked under the tables. Carla and Sophie checked the teacher's desk. Charlie and Baby Five looked in the toilets and the three other baby dolls checked where the bricks were kept.
They searched for two hours, but they couldn't find Greta. "Perhaps one of the children took her home," Clown suggested.

9 June In the sand pit

The other dolls spent the whole night looking for Greta. Carla, Sophie, Charlie, Clown and the five babies were so tired that they were all asleep when the teacher arrived at school.

"Hey sleepy-heads!" she shouted.

The dolls woke up right away.

"Cock-a-doodle-do. It's morning!" giggled someone.

It was Greta!

"Greta! Where were you? We looked all over for you," shouted the dolls.

"I was outside," explained Greta. "I spent the night in the sandpit. One of the children took me there but forgot to bring me back again."

10 June Big black monster

"Weren't you scared of the dark?" Carla asked.

"Not at first," said Greta, "but in the middle of the night a big black monster suddenly came up to me. He sniffed me and opened his mouth. I was terrified when I saw all those sharp teeth!"

"Stop it Greta! This story is too frightening!"

Carla and Sophie closed their eyes.

"Well," continued Greta, "I heard a whistle and the monster left. I could see from the street lamp that it was Mr Johnson's dog." Fortunately Mr Johnson's dog was very lovable.

11 June **Teacher's idea**

The infants were sitting in a big circle. They were very quiet because Miss Jenkins had something to tell them.
"Last night," she said, "I had an idea. How would you like to have a doll as a lodger?" The children didn't understand what a lodger was. The teacher explained.
"A lodger is someone who comes to stay with you. You could take it in turns to take a doll home with you for a week. During that week you would have to take good care of the doll. When you bring it back, it should look exactly the same."
"Can we take the dolls to bed with us?" the children asked.
"Yes, you can," said Miss Jenkins with a smile.

12 June **Whose turn is it?**

The children were excited at the thought of taking a doll home for a week. But the problem was who would be the first to take the doll home? The children wanted to know. They started arguing.
Quiet everyone!" shouted Miss Jenkins. "We're not going to argue about this. The first person will be the youngest, and then the second youngest will be next. The last one will be the oldest pupil. That is Bart. Bart will have to wait a long time, but because he is a big boy, I am sure he can manage that."

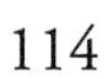

13 June **Louisa**

Louisa was the youngest child. She was just four years old and she had only been at the nursery school for a few days. Louisa was the first to take a doll home with her. She was allowed to choose which doll she would take from the dolls' corner.
She couldn't decide. Greta was lovely and the clown was so funny, but perhaps a baby doll would be best, or perhaps not? The dolls were on their best behaviour. They all wanted to be the lodger. Finally, Louisa chose Carla, because of her pretty dark curls.

14 June **Two beds?**

Louisa put Carla in her rucksack. Carla couldn't wait to find out what Louisa's bedroom was like. She was so excited. She peeped over the top of the rucksack when they walked into Louisa's room. There were two beds in Louisa's room. Carla wondered why.
"There," said Louisa. "This is my bed and that is my brother Carl's bed."
"Carl!" Carla was horrified.
She had completely forgotten that Carl was Louisa's brother.
That nuisance Carl.
He was always trouble!

15 June **Singing**

Even though the dolls in the dolls' corner sometimes got a bit fed up, they really liked it at the nursery school. At least one of the children wanted to play with them each day. Most of the children played nice games with them. Sometimes the children had to do other things like cutting things out of magazines and making pretty pictures to take home with them.
Even the dolls liked it at school. They could watch the children from their corner. They liked it best when the children sang songs. They put their chairs in a circle and sang in time with their teacher.
Very, very softly, without letting the children or the teacher hear them, the dolls sung along with them.

16 June Thirty sweet little voices

Thirty sweet little voices,
Sing songs of things happy and bright,
Of the sun and the moon, the stars and the trees,
The world covered in light.

Thirty sweet little voices,
Sing about good and not bad,
Their favourite tunes and verses,
Nothing to make you sad.

17 June Wooden tummy

The infants had learned a pretty song. It was one of those songs that stay in your head the whole day. You keep singing it. The dolls kept singing their new song. In the evening, when the children were in bed, the dolls were singing again. One of the baby dolls suddenly stopped singing.

"Listen," he said to Baby Two.

"Have you heard how beautifully Charlie sings?" Baby Two listened to Charlie. It was true. Charlie was singing so beautifully that everyone stopped to listen to him.

Charlie blushed and said, "It's because I have a wooden tummy that the sound is so sweet."

18 June What a mess!

John left Clown on the table while he did his painting and pasting. Clown soon had one arm in the pot of paste and the other in the red paint. He was in a bit of a state. Scraps of paper were stuck to his hair. When Miss Jenkins saw him, she was angry. "John! Look at Clown. He's so messy. How would you like it if you looked like him?" She looked more closely at John. He had paint on his clothes and scraps of paper stuck to his hair. John was just as untidy as Clown!

19 June In the wash

That evening, Miss Jenkins took Clown home with her and gave him a wash. She wasn't sure she'd be able to get him as clean as before. Clown was in a bucket, up to his ears in soapy water. He didn't mind that too much, but when the teacher pushed his head under the water a few times, he coughed and spluttered. It felt dreadful, but he knew she was trying to get his head clean too. She left Clown to soak all night. The next morning, he was as good as new. She pegged him on the line to dry.

20 June **Strange washing**

What strange washing
Is hanging on the line?
It has a head and feet as well,
It's laughing in the sunshine.
The wash is, yes you've guessed,
The newly laundered clown.
He spent a whole night soaking,
But it doesn't get him down.

21 June **Jealous**

Clown looked clean once more,
Teacher washed him at home,
"Me too please," said Baby One,
"Why choose him alone?"

22 June **Birthday**

It was Sandra's birthday. She was five years old. Sandra was allowed to choose whatever she wanted to play with. She didn't have to think about it for long, because she had got a dolls' pram for her birthday. She had brought it to school to show her teacher. She wanted to play with it in the dolls' corner. Bart could play too.

23 June **Doll's pram**

When Sandra and Bart pushed the pram into the dolls' corner, the dolls were amazed when they saw it. It was bright and colourful with a lovely blue hood and white wheels. It even had a mattress and a blanket. All the dolls hoped that Sandra and Bart would take them for a ride in it.

24 June Inching forward

They wished they could speak and let Sandra know how much they wanted a ride in the pram. But children can't understand what dolls say. "Perhaps if I think really hard," hoped Clown. "I try that all the time. It doesn't work," Carla said glumly. The baby dolls were silent. They started to creep forward, pushing and shoving a little. The other dolls didn't notice though. As soon as they realised what the babies were doing, they were already underneath the pram!

25 June Already taken!

The baby dolls and Greta, Carla, Clown and Sophie were arguing. "I want to go in the dolls' pram!" "No me!" Because they were squabbling so much, they didn't notice that someone was looking over the side of the pram. "What's going on?" said a voice from the pram. Startled, the dolls looked up to see two twinkling big brown eyes and a pretty face surrounded by a mass of curls. There was already a doll in the dolls' pram. There had been no point in arguing. The doll in the pram asked them all, "Will you be my friends? Then you can all take it in turns to ride in the pram."

26 June A real baby

Lucy and Kim were playing together next to the dolls' corner. Lucy was carrying a baby doll and was feeding it with a bottle. Kim was bored.
"I don't think much of baby dolls," she said.
"I think real babies are much nicer!"
Lucy didn't understand Kim. Lucy shrugged her shoulders and carried on playing with her doll.
"We've got a real baby at home," Kim said. "It's so sweet. I think the baby dolls are stupid."
The baby dolls were shocked. Didn't the children want to play with them anymore?

27 June What's wrong with us?

The babies were worried when they heard Kim say that baby dolls were stupid. What was wrong with them?
Baby One said, "Perhaps we aren't soft enough?"
Baby Two thought their clothes weren't pretty enough.
Baby Three said, "In the shops they now sell babies that really cry!"
Baby Four sighed, "And dolls with batteries."
Baby Five just cried.
Then they heard Kim say to Lucy, "My baby sister is so funny. Sometimes she goes red in the face and then five minutes later her nappy is dirty!"
So that was it. The baby dolls were relieved. Now they knew what they had to do!

28 June **Nappy alert!**

"What are all the baby dolls up to?" Clown asked Greta.

"Don't you know?" laughed Greta.

"No," replied Clown, who was getting more and more curious. "Tell me!"

"Those stupid baby dolls thought the children didn't like them any more. Then they heard a girl say that real babies are much nicer. Real babies go red in the face and fill their nappies. Now five of the baby dolls are practising. They are trying to see who can go the reddest!"

Clown couldn't believe it and he started to laugh. He laughed until he had to clutch his tummy with his hands. Tears streamed down his cheeks. "Ha, ha, ha! It doesn't matter how red they go – they will never fill their nappies!"

29 June **Holiday**

Carla, Greta, Clown, Sophia, Charlie and the five baby dolls were sitting on the window sill. Feeling miserable, they gazed out of the window. They watched the children skipping off home with their mothers or fathers.

"Now we'll be on our own for six weeks," sighed Greta. "I hate the summer holidays!" The other dolls sighed. They would really miss the children. Then Charlie banged his wooden arms together to get their attention.

"If we spend the whole six weeks whining, the holiday will go so slowly. Come on, let's have some fun. Let's play the instruments. Music will cheer us up!"

30 June

A smiling heart

Oh come on do,
Stop whining so,
Nobody at all
Will want to know.
If on you moan,
Never smiling all day,
"You are a real grump",
All your friends will say.

So buck up do,
Look around you with a smile,
It will turn out to be
A wonder in a while.
Once you stop being glum,
You can think about good things,
And all the joy and happiness
A smiling heart brings.

1 July **Theo**

Theo was a marionette. Or rather he had been a marionette until his strings got broken. Theo used to be famous, appearing every day in the puppet theatre with other marionettes. The puppeteer who worked his strings was an old man and his hands began to tremble. When Theo's strings had broken, the old man couldn't replace them. For a while, Theo had performed with only one arm. When the strings for his legs also got broken, he had to stop for good.

2 July **Bits and pieces**

Theo's wooden face was sad. He was scared to move. Theo was afraid that he would fall apart if he should move. That had already happened. His right arm and his legs had fallen off. Theo hadn't seen the old puppeteer for a long time. The other puppets hadn't seen him either. "Soon I'll just be a broken old marionette, made of bits and pieces," Theo muttered quietly. "Who will help me? I'm a puppet, not a puzzle."

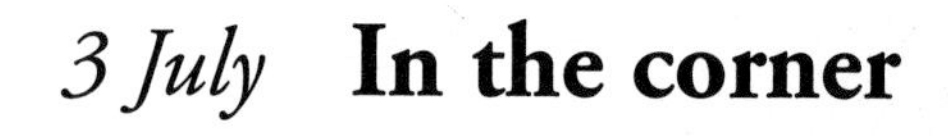

3 July In the corner

It was quiet in the puppet theatre. The play had finished and the people had gone home. Theo was sitting in a dusty junk room where all the bits and pieces were stored. He had been listening to the performance. He knew from the music which puppet play was on. Today's play was about a poor boy who had never been lucky. Not until he was visited by a fairy. The fairy granted him three wishes. The young boy lived a long and happy life.

4 July If I could make a wish

"Oh, if only I could make a wish," thought Theo. He knew just what he would wish for. He would wish for new strings so that he could move again like the other marionettes. He wanted to be back on the stage. Suddenly he heard a sound like a rocket. The dark corner glowed and shimmered. A pale blue figure floated in the middle of the shimmering light.
"Hello Theo," said the strange figure. "I am Xalandra the fairy. I hear that you want to make a wish."
Theo was astonished.

5 July **The fairy**

Theo couldn't believe his marionette's eyes. There was a fairy floating in front of him and the fairy said he could make a wish.
"Dear, dear fairy, can you help me?" he asked, his voice trembling.
"Tell me your wish and I shall make it come true," the fairy smiled.
Theo cleared his throat, tried not to be frightened and said, "I wish ... I wish that I could make both grown-ups and children happy. But to do that, my strings have to be mended. Is that possible?" The fairy nodded and smiled.

6 July **Please?**

Dearest lovely fairy,
Help me in my need,
Pick up all my pieces,
This is all I plead.

Oh my dear fairy,
Though I am made from trees,
I need new strings a-stringing,
Oh won't you help me please?

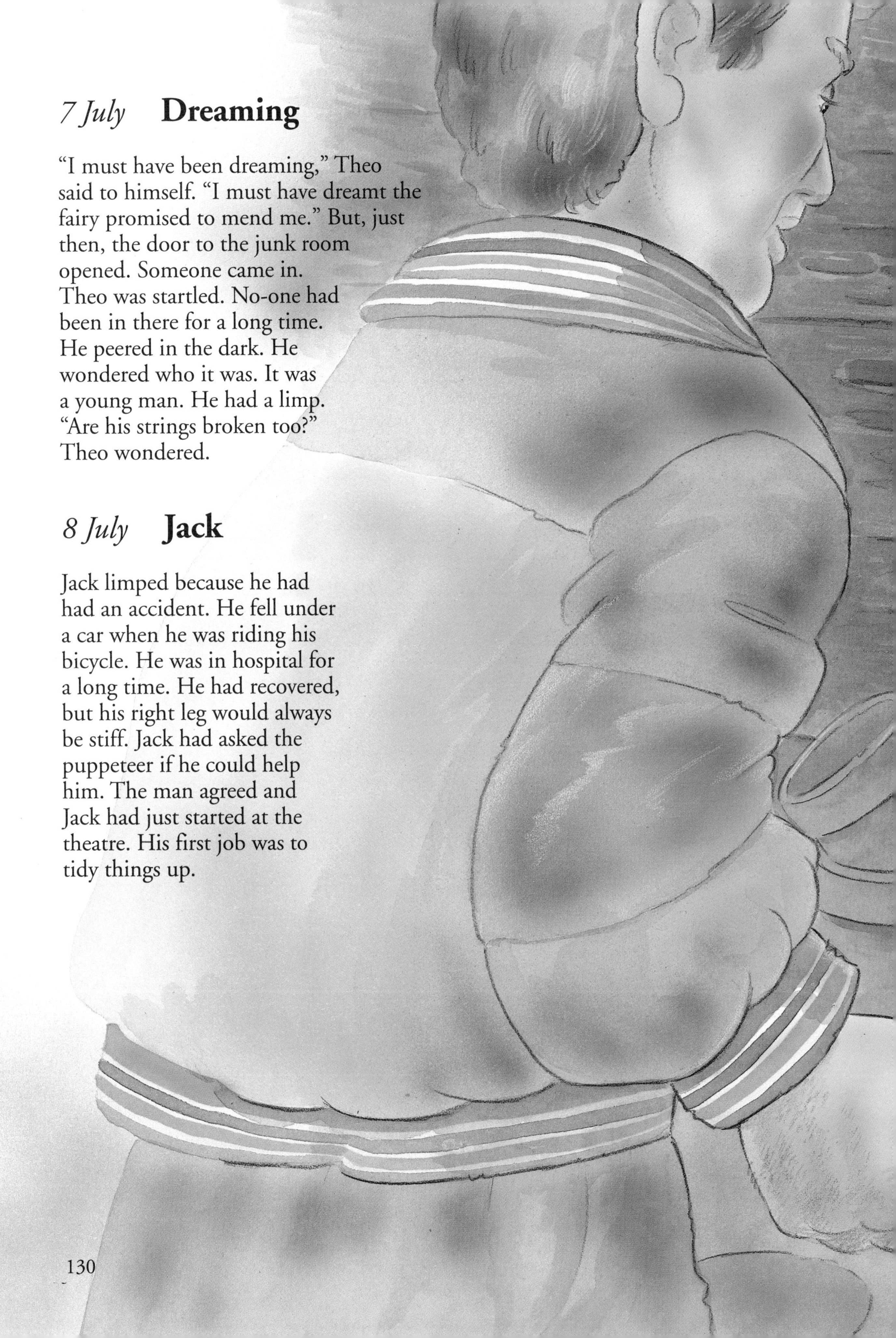

7 July **Dreaming**

"I must have been dreaming," Theo said to himself. "I must have dreamt the fairy promised to mend me." But, just then, the door to the junk room opened. Someone came in. Theo was startled. No-one had been in there for a long time. He peered in the dark. He wondered who it was. It was a young man. He had a limp. "Are his strings broken too?" Theo wondered.

8 July **Jack**

Jack limped because he had had an accident. He fell under a car when he was riding his bicycle. He was in hospital for a long time. He had recovered, but his right leg would always be stiff. Jack had asked the puppeteer if he could help him. The man agreed and Jack had just started at the theatre. His first job was to tidy things up.

9 July **Elves?**

When Jack pushed open the door to the junk room, he muttered "Gosh, it's dark. I can't see a thing." He put his hands in front of him to feel his way around.
He touched an old jacket, a chair and then a tiny hand.
"Oh! What's that?" Jack was startled. "Are their mice in here?" He decided to fetch a torch.

10 July **A new owner?**

Jack returned to the junk room with a torch. He shone the light on the spot where he had felt a tiny hand.
"Ha!" Jack laughed. "It's an old marionette. Oh poor old thing is in pieces. I'll ask the puppet master if I can have him. Maybe I'll be able to put him together again." Jack put all the pieces in a plastic bag and went to see the puppet master.

11 July **Help!**

Oh poor Theo. He didn't understand that Jack wanted to help him. He only knew that a big person came and shoved him in a bag. Then the bag moved. He didn't know that Jack had a limp and he couldn't understand that this meant he would be jostled around. Theo's right foot was stuck in his left ear. He was really frightened as Jack climbed some stairs. Oh poor marionette. He didn't realise that Jack was planning to put him together again.

12 July **Fingers and thumbs**

Back home, Jack turned on the light at his table. He needed to concentrate on which pieces fitted where. It was very puzzling. Putting all the pieces together wouldn't be easy, but he was determined to do it.

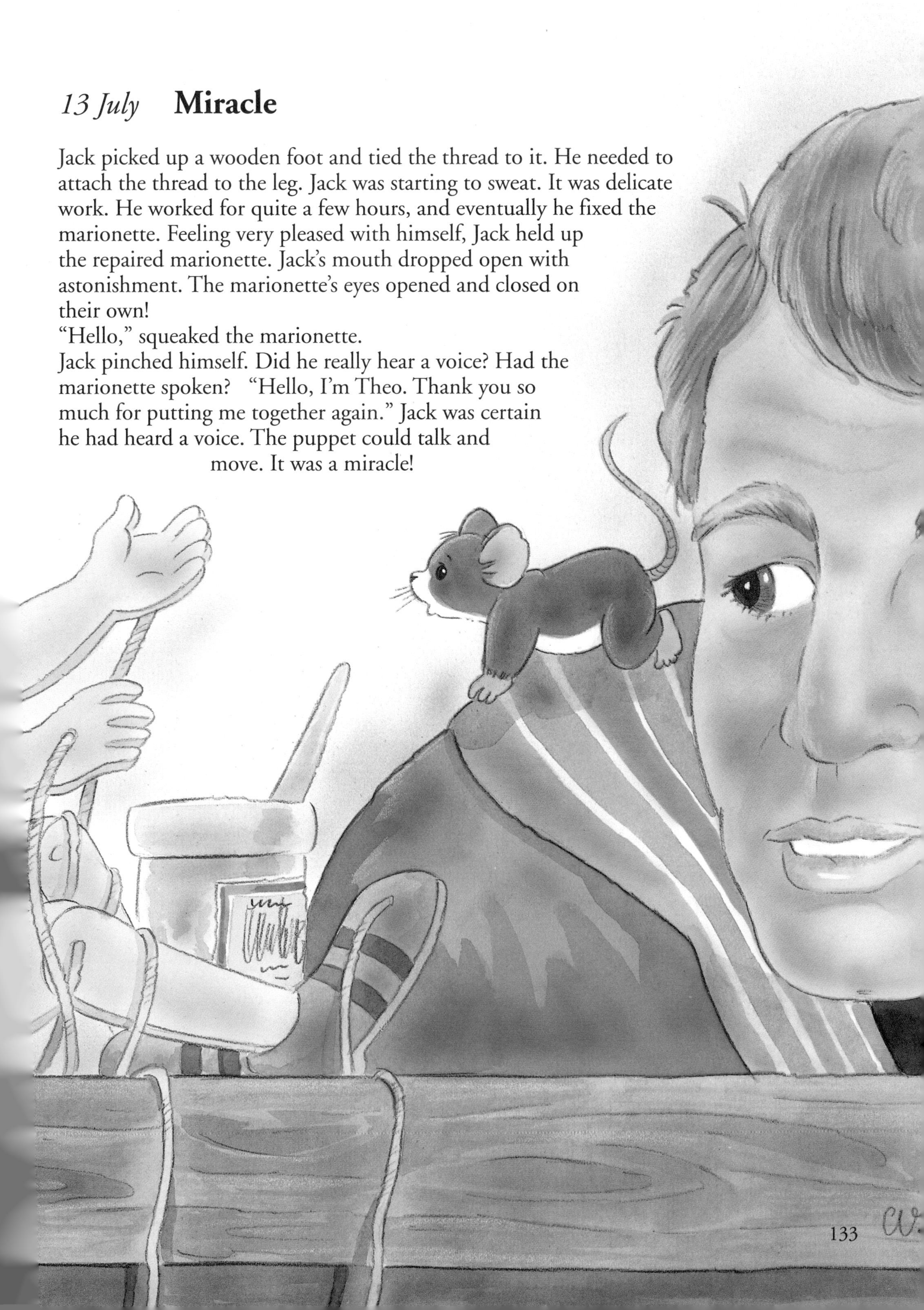

13 July **Miracle**

Jack picked up a wooden foot and tied the thread to it. He needed to attach the thread to the leg. Jack was starting to sweat. It was delicate work. He worked for quite a few hours, and eventually he fixed the marionette. Feeling very pleased with himself, Jack held up the repaired marionette. Jack's mouth dropped open with astonishment. The marionette's eyes opened and closed on their own!

"Hello," squeaked the marionette.

Jack pinched himself. Did he really hear a voice? Had the marionette spoken? "Hello, I'm Theo. Thank you so much for putting me together again." Jack was certain he had heard a voice. The puppet could talk and move. It was a miracle!

14 July Talking puppet

Jack was absolutely stunned.
"H .. h .. how come you can talk?"
Jack stuttered.
The marionette scratched his head.
"I don't really know. When I was in
the junk room, I was visited by a fairy.
Perhaps she has bewitched me."
Talking puppets, fairies ... Jack was
imagining what a puppet like this
could do. He could perform all over
the world, perhaps even appear on
television! Jack imagined himself as
a world-famous puppeteer.

15 July Come and see

Come and see,
Come and see,
The most amazing thing you've ever seen,
Greater than a flying machine,
Stranger than a dinosaur,
A puppet talking, and what's more,
He dances without the aid of man,
And does things that no other puppet can,
His picture was there on the front page
It's made him now the latest rage.

16 July **Would you like to do that?**

"No Jack!" Theo said. "No-one must know that I can talk and move on my own. It's a secret between me and you." Jack was amazed. Could the puppet read his mind? "Yes Jack, I can," nodded Theo. "The fairy who bewitched me made me like this. But she did it for a reason. She wanted me to help adults and children. That's why I can look right into people's hearts. I know if someone is sad or happy."

"But what's the point of that?" Jack asked. "If you can't tell anyone?"

"That's why I need you Jack," explained the puppet. "You must pretend to be my puppeteer. You will take me to see people. You will hold my strings. Would you like to do that?"

17 July **Jack's help**

Jack didn't have to think about it for long. He knew that Theo wanted to help people forget their problems for a little while. Jack knew what being sad was like. He was very depressed about his leg after the accident. He wept for a long time. He needed something then to lift his spirits.

"Of course I will help you Theo!" he beamed.

"We will set off tomorrow!"

18 July **Ice-cream shop**

Jack was walking along a busy street. Theo was in his rucksack. It was a warm summer's day and the ice-cream shop on the corner was doing good business. But why was a little girl crying in front of the shop? Jack walked up to her and asked, "What's the matter? Have you lost your mother and father?"
The girl was frightened. Jack didn't want to scare her. Suddenly Theo nudged him in the back. He wanted to get out of the rucksack. Jack thought that was a good idea. Perhaps the girl wouldn't be so frightened of Theo.

19 July **The dancing puppet**

Jack took Theo out of the bag. The puppet jumped down on to the street and skipped over to the little girl. The child laughed at the funny puppet.
The puppet danced around her and started to act. Jack decided that the best thing to do was to fetch a police officer from the local police station. Luckily when he got to the station, the little girl's parents were there. Jack and the police officer then took them straight back to the ice-cream shop.

20 July All the praise

The police officer was very pleased with Jack. "You acted very sensibly and honestly Jack. The little girl's parents were so worried." When the police officer had left, Jack whispered, "You helped the little girl too, not just me, but I get all the praise. Aren't you a bit annoyed about that?" Theo shook his head. "Not at all. The only thing that is important is that we helped the little girl."

21 July Teasing

Teasing really is not fair,
And is usually done,
By a crowd of horrid people
Ganging up on just one.
Some people are different,
Different to the rest,
Yet nasty people pick on them,
They really are a pest.
Teasing, bullying, calling names,
It is horrid to endure it,
Yet the most stupid of them all
Are the brainless twits who do it.

22 July Poor Martin

Martin was walking home. His house was only a few streets away from school. He could walk back in two minutes. But it took Martin much longer. Martin was frightened of a group of big boys who teased and bullied him. Martin preferred to walk the long way round. Usually then he avoided them. "Just around the corner and I'll be home," he mumbled to himself. He was about to breathe a sigh of relief but ... there they were. They were real bullies. Martin turned and ran. But the boys weren't going to leave him alone and they chased after him.

23 July Hiding-place

Martin ran as if his life depended on it. The boys were much bigger than him. Fortunately Martin knew a hiding-place nearby. If he was quick enough, he could hide. He got there – just in time! But Martin was shocked. There was someone in his hiding-place. A puppeteer with a marionette.
"Hello Martin," said the puppeteer. "Nasty boys aren't they? Would you like to teach them a lesson?" Martin was surprised, but he nodded. How did the puppeteer know his name?

24 July A show

Jack and Theo had decided to teach the boys who were bullying Martin a lesson. They went to Martin's school and offered to perform a show for all the children there. After the break all the children waited in the gymnasium. They were looking forward to the show. They wondered what it would be about.
It was a play about a group of bigger boys who teased and bullied a boy who was much smaller than they were. Without naming names, everyone knew who the play was about. The bullies felt guilty and embarrassed. From now on Martin would be able to walk home in peace.

25 July How clever!

Sometimes Theo sat on Jack's shoulders. "How clever that boy is," people said. "He can carry the puppet on his shoulders and still make him move!"
Jack and Theo giggled. If only people knew ... but no-one was to know that Theo could talk and move himself.

26 July Long nose

Theo was feeling a bit mischievous today. He was sitting on Jack's shoulders with his legs dangling over them. Suddenly his eyes lit up and his nose got longer.
Of course people thought that Jack was making Theo do that. They loved it. "As long as the people laugh at your antics, I don't mind," muttered Jack. "But if they get angry, they might turn nasty on me ... not on you. That's what I'm worried about."

27 July The old man

"Look!" pointed Jack. "I wonder what those people are looking at. Let's take a look." Jack carefully made his way through the crowd until he was at the front. Standing there was an old man who was playing an accordion. He had put his hat on the ground inviting anyone who liked his music to give him some money. But there was hardly any money in the hat. Just a few pennies.

28 July Theo's jig

Jack and Theo listened to the musician. He was playing old melodies on his accordion.

"Can you play a jig sir?" Jack asked the old man. Theo danced to the music. Jack was struggling to stop the strings getting in a tangle. But when Theo stopped dancing, there was a lot more money in the musician's hat. He would be able to eat in a restaurant for a week.

29 July I'm useless

"Hey Jack, why are you looking so miserable today?" Theo asked. "What's the matter with you?" Jack shrugged his shoulders. He didn't really know. He felt miserable when he got out of bed that morning and his mood wouldn't go away.
"Perhaps it's because I feel so useless. I can't do much with my gammy leg."
Theo looked at him in surprise. "Useless?" Theo couldn't understand what Jack meant.
"No. You, at least, make people happy. But me ... I just pretend to hold your strings. I'm not much use on my own. I don't make anyone happy." Theo sighed.
"That just isn't true Jack. You have made somebody very, very happy."
Who do you think Theo was talking about?

30 July Big Kiss

"Have I made someone happy?" Jack asked Theo. Theo nodded. "Extremely happy," he said. Jack hadn't got a clue who he meant. "Can't you guess?" Theo asked. Jack shook his head. "Why, me of course!" Theo laughed. "You put me together again. Without you, I would still be in the junk room. It's true, isn't it?"
"I suppose so. Yes, I suppose you are right!" Jack felt a bit better. Perhaps he had been some use. He picked up Theo and gave him a big kiss on his wooden nose.

31 July

Hooray

Hip hip hooray,
I would so like to say,
How you are a hero to me,
My friend I hope you'll always be.

Hip hip hoorah,
You've been loyal, good by far,
Whenever I was upset and down,
You were always there to stop my frown.

No better friend have I ever had,
For your honesty I'm always glad,
So hip hip hooray,
Friendship will last every day.

1 August An accident

Sarah White was sitting at the table. She was just about to put some bread and jam in her mouth when ... crash! Sarah jumped up and ran to the window. She saw a big lorry and it had turned over. Sarah ran outside because the driver might have been hurt. Perhaps she could help.

2 August The lorry's load

The lorry was badly dented and the tailboard at the back of the lorry had broken off. When Sarah reached the lorry, the driver was standing next to it. Fortunately he wasn't hurt. Sarah was curious and walked to the back. What was in it? She stood and stared. The load had fallen on the road. Hundreds of dolls – large dolls, small dolls, fat dolls, skinny dolls - were lying there. Sarah had never seen so many dolls before.

3 August Two hundred eyes

Two hundred eyes looked up at little Sarah as if they were asking her for help.
"Don't just stand there," they seemed to be saying. "Save us from this hard, cold road. Our driver is quite hopeless and he doesn't know what to do!"
Sarah walked over to the driver and offered to help. "If you would like to telephone anyone, you could use the one at our house. I will ask my mother."

4 August What about the dolls?

The driver was pleased. "Oh, yes please." Sarah took him to her house and her mother took him to the telephone. "Who will you call?" Sarah asked. "The police?" The man nodded. "And I'll ask for a recovery truck too."
"Who is going to look after the dolls?" asked Sarah. The man hadn't thought about them.
"But the dolls are scattered all over the road. You can't just leave them there." The man shrugged his shoulders. "I'll have to leave them there for the time being," he said. Sarah was horrified.

5 August Lots of friends

Sarah wasn't prepared to leave all those poor dolls lying on the road. She would have to do something about it. She had an idea. She had lots of friends. She was sure they would help. Sarah put on her coat. She was going to see her friends.

6 August To the rescue

When the police arrived at the scene of the accident, there were lots of children there. Sarah had rounded up all her friends. They had collected all the dolls that had been lying on the road. One of the police officers took off his jacket and gave the children a hand. "It's a shame to leave all those dolls just lying there," he said.

7 August On the front page

At the scene of the overturned lorry,
Equipped with his camera and pen,
Is a man from the local paper,
Who looks so surprised when
He sees what the children are doing,
Amid all the metal and glass.
"This will make tonight's 'Late Final',
It's too good a story to pass."
'Children rescue dolls'
Was the headline that night,
The children's good work
Was certainly proved right.
The man took a picture of Sarah,
And was quick to ask her age,
For the rescue was her idea,
And now she is on the front page.

8 August A heroine

There was a big photograph of Sarah in the evening paper. Underneath, in small print, were the words, "Small girl rescues dolls from overturned lorry."
"Well Sarah," said her father. "You are a real heroine. Look! You're in the paper!"
She looked at the photograph showing her standing among all the dolls. She felt quite proud. Not everybody got in the newspaper. But she was truthful. "I didn't do it on my own. All my friends helped and even a nice police officer."
Father gave her a big kiss. Her parents were so proud of her.

9 August An invitation

The telephone was ringing.
"Hello, Sarah White here," Sarah answered as her parents had taught her. "Hello Sarah," someone said. "You must be the little girl who saved the dolls?" "Yes," replied Sarah. "I'm the owner of a toy shop. The lorry driver was delivering the dolls to me when the accident happened. I would like to thank you for rescuing my dolls. Would you like to come to my shop for a day?" "I'd love to," says Sarah, "but ..." "If your mummy and daddy agree of course," said the shop owner. Sarah then asked shyly, "Could my friends come too? They helped me and ..." "Of course," said the shop owner.

10 August In the toy shop

Sarah White and her friends were standing in the middle of the big toy shop. There were all sorts of toys there. Trains, bricks, balls, dolls, board games. There was so much, it was hard to remember it all. But the children wanted just one thing. They wanted to go to the doll department. They want to see the dolls they had rescued. They followed the owner to the dolls.
"Look, there they are!" the children shouted. "There's the doll with the blonde hair. And here's one of the rag dolls." And do you know what was strange? It seemed as though the dolls recognised the children too.

11 August **Mama**

There were at least a hundred dolls on the shelves in the doll department. A hundred? No, a thousand! Perhaps even a million. Sarah was so excited. She spotted a sweet doll. Sarah carefully lifted it off the shelf and stroked its tummy.
"Mama!" it said.
The doll could talk! "No," Sarah laughed. "I'm not your mummy."
Sarah knew that the doll couldn't talk really. There was a little machine inside it that made it talk. But when she put the doll back on the shelf and walked away, she heard the doll say "Mama" again. How strange!

12 August **Rustle, rustle**

The dolls all knew who Sarah was. She had rescued them.
"I would love to live with Sarah," sighed Jacko the rag doll. "Me too," sighed Nelly the baby doll next to him. "We must try to attract her attention," suggested Jacko.
"But what can we do? People can't hear what we say," replied Nelly.
"What if we make our clothes rustle?" Jacko suggested. "We could try, but we will have to rustle very hard. There is so much noise in the shop she might not hear us."

13 August **Ghosts?**

Sarah thought that strange things were happening at the toy shop. A baby doll had said "Mama" without being touched and now there was a strange rustling sound coming from the dolls. Sarah didn't realise how grateful the dolls were and how much they wanted to thank her.
"Are there ghosts in this place?" Sarah mumbled to herself.

14 August **Surprise**

"Come here, Sarah," said the shop owner. "And bring your friends with you." The children followed him. "I think you all did a marvellous job rescuing the dolls from the overturned lorry. I want to thank each and every one of you. Please pick any doll you want." The children were thrilled. "Can we keep it?" "And can we choose *any* one?" "And..." "And..." The toy shop owner hadn't been prepared for all these questions. He put his hands over his ears and laughed.

15 August **Difficult to choose**

Sarah's wish had come true. She could choose any doll she wanted. But which one should she have, because there were so many lovely dolls. A rag doll had a happy smile. And a baby doll was so sweet, and the doll with the long blonde plaits was gorgeous.
"Gosh, it's so hard to choose," sighed Sarah. "I would like to take them all home with me." But she couldn't do that, and, besides, she would never fit them all in her room!

16 August

Choose me, choose me!

All the dolls in the toy shop were nervous. Sarah could choose whichever one she wanted. They all hoped she would choose them. Jacko the rag doll wasn't sure what else he could do to get her attention.

"Sarah, Sarah, choose me!" he shouted in doll talk. Silly Jacko. He knew that people couldn't hear doll talk. Jacko leaned forward. Oh take care! You will fall Jacko. Too late! With a thud, Jacko fell under the shelf. Sarah would never find him there.

17 August

The prettiest

"I suppose you lot can always try,"
said Patricia the china doll.
"I know for certain that Sarah will choose me. After all, I am the prettiest doll in the shop." Patricia shook her brown ringlets and puffed up her lace dress.
When Sarah passed her, Patricia winked at her with her large green eyes.
"That didn't help," laughed the other dolls.
"You're still on the shelf Patricia."
"Just wait a moment," Patricia said angrily, "and you'll see."
The dolls watched nervously. Would Sarah choose conceited Patricia or not?

18 August

Conceited Patricia

Patricia the china doll,
Gives herself airs and graces,
Arrogantly she is quite sure,
She has the prettiest of faces.
She is quite certain that Sarah will
Think her quite the best
"You lot do not stand a chance,"
She mocks all the rest.
"No other doll within the store
Has a silk dress like this."
If you could hear the dolly's talk,
You'd surely hear them hiss.

19 August **Stuck-up thing**

Sarah looked at the china dolls. They were very pretty, but she didn't think they would be much fun to play with.

"I want a doll I can really cuddle," Sarah decided and walked on.

"What!" Patricia the china doll couldn't believe it! If china dolls could blush, Patricia would have been the colour of a tomato. She was so angry.

"That girl needs glasses!" she shouted angrily.

"Brilliant!" thought Nelly the baby doll.

"Stuck-up thing," giggled Jacko from underneath the shelf.

20 August **A fool**

Patricia thought Sarah was a fool. "What girl would walk past the prettiest doll in the whole shop?" she thought. She grumbled and groaned. "If Sarah doesn't want me, I don't want her! I can't bear to look at her," she hissed. In fury she tried to twist her head round. But china dolls are stiff. They can't turn their heads. Craaacck! The china shattered into a thousand pieces. Oh dear Patricia. Sarah wasn't the foolish one. No-one would want a broken china doll.

21 August

Flip and Flop

In one corner of the toy shop there were clowns. They looked so cheerful in their brightly coloured jackets. Flip and Flop were sitting together. You could tell that they belonged together. They were practically identical, but Flip had a red hat and Flop had a blue one. Flip's jacket was blue and Flop's was red. Flip's trousers were yellow with green spots and Flop's were green with yellow spots. They had the same shoes - floppy purple clown's shoes, and they both had very cheeky eyes!

22 August

Wobblebot

Flip and Flop loved to play practical jokes. Mr Bouncy Ball knew what they got up to.
"Look here Mr Bouncy Ball," whispered Flop in one ear.
"No, here" whispered Flip in the other ear.
Mr Bouncy Ball didn't have legs, just a big round body like a bowling ball. Once he started wobbling from one side to the other, he couldn't stop. He could wobble for a quarter of an hour. Flip and Flop were making Mr Bouncy Ball wobble.
They laughed and laughed.
"There's a better name for you than Bouncy Ball," laughed Flip.
"You ought to be called Mr Wobblebot," joked Flop.

23 August **Fright**

Sarah laughed when she saw the clowns. “What about one of those two with the big floppy shoes?” she thought. Flip and Flop were worried. They liked Sarah, but they couldn’t be parted. They wanted to stay together forever.
“If Sarah chooses you,” sighed Flop, “I will be so sad.”
Flip looked as though he was going to cry. “That’s odd,” thought Sarah, “clowns are supposed to be cheerful. No, I wouldn’t choose a sad clown.”
“Phew!” Flip and Flop heaved a sigh of relief.

24 August

Eyes shut

"Is it difficult to choose?" the owner of the toy shop asked Sarah.
"Yes," replied Sarah. "I like all your dolls."
"Well, take another good look," he said. "But remember, the shop closes in half an hour. You need to choose by then." Sarah nodded. She went to have another look.
"If I still don't know," she said, "I will choose with my eyes shut."

25 August

That's the one

All Sarah's friends had chosen their dolls. One had a baby doll that could really wet the bed. Another had a doll with long blonde plaits. Sarah's neighbour had an enormous doll in her arms.
"Look she can really walk!" cried the girl.
Sarah was the only one who hadn't chosen. Suddenly she saw a funny doll with red plaits. "That's the one!" Sarah shouted.
"I know that doll. She was lying in the middle of the road when the lorry turned over. That was the first doll I saw!"

26 August **Pipi**

"Are you sure?" the owner asked Sarah and laughed. "Yes," she answered. "I rescued this doll from the street. I remember the red plaits." She wanted to take this doll as a reminder of the day. Pipi couldn't believe her luck. She used to hate her red hair. She thought it was awful. But because of her funny red plaits, Sarah had chosen her. Red hair was lucky after all.

27 August

Be mine

Will you always be mine?
Don't let me guess.
Please give me your answer now,
Oh do let it be yes.
Though we met but recently,
I think of you all the day,
I'm certain that I love you,
In every possible way.

28 August Going home

Sarah was holding Pipi as they drove home with her parents.
"Going home. That sounds good," Pipi was happy. "Finally I have a real home."
"Look Pipi, that's where I live," Sarah told her. She held Pipi up to the window so that she could look out. Pipi stared. "That's my bedroom," said Sarah pointing to one of the windows upstairs.

29 August **A friend**

Sarah's room wasn't big, but it was cosy. Pipi had been given the best place to sleep - on the bed.
"Nice and soft for my bottom," sighed Pipi happily.
"Who are you?" said a deep voice above her.
Pipi looked up and saw a large brown teddy bear. He was looking at her with curiosity.
"I'm Pipi and I have come here to live," Pipi replied.
Teddy bear's voice boomed out.
"Welcome Pipi. I am Fluff and I already live here. I hope we can be friends. When Sarah sleeps we can play together and talk."
"That would be nice," replied Pipi.
"Oh, I'm so lucky. Now I've got a new home and also a friend."

30 August **To bed**

Sarah was about to go to bed. She had cleaned her teeth. After putting on her pyjamas, she crept under the covers. Sarah laid Pipi next to her under the sheets "Oh wait a moment, I nearly forgot Fluff."
She got out of bed and carefully picked up her teddy. She gave him a kiss on the top of his bear head. "You belong in bed with me too," she said to him as she stroked his head.
Sarah could only get to sleep when she had her teddy and her doll with her in bed.

31 August **Ready for bed**

Pipi, Fluff and Sarah
Are ready now for bed.
Snuggling under the sheets,
The last to sleep is Ted.

Pipi has been quite excited,
A new home in just one day.
In between Sarah and Ted,
She wouldn't have it any other way.

1 September **Aunt Celia**

Some children don't like visiting elderly aunts on a Sunday afternoon because their houses are really tidy and they never have any toys to play with. But twins Nina and Nick liked visiting their aunt. Their aunt was very large and she tied up her snowy-white hair in a bun. Her name was Celia. Aunt Celia had some beautiful things. The nicest of all was the music box with the ballet dancer. The twins could play anywhere in the house as long as they were careful.

2 September **Yummy**

Aunt Celia was waiting for them by the door. The twins had come with their parents.
"Hello my dears," she said with a chuckle.
"Hi Aunt Celia!" cried Nina and Nick.
"Have you got something yummy for tea?"
Aunt closes her eyes. "Now let's see. Oh food, oh dear no, I've forgotten that."
Nina and Norris laughed. Aunt Celia always played this game. She always teased them. There would be something really delicious for tea they were sure.

3 September

Mantelpiece

There were some lovely old things on Aunt Celia's mantelpiece. There were two porcelain angels, one holding a harp and the other a flute. When the twins had finished their tea, they asked politely. "May we play with the music box Aunt Celia?" "Of course you may, my dears."

4 September

Music box

Music box, music box,
Let your tune ring.
When your lid's open,
Our hearts start to sing.
When your tune plays,
A ballerina spins round.
We watch her with awe,
Hardly making a sound.

5 September

Princess Ballerina

Aunt Celia's music box was no ordinary music box. You didn't just wind it up and a tune played. Inside Aunt Celia's music box there was a ballerina. When you opened the lid, she popped up and danced in time with the music. "Isn't she lovely?" sighed Nina to her brother. "She is Princess Ballerina."

6 September

Ballet shoes

The little doll in the music box heard what the children said about her. She was so pleased that the children had called her a ballerina. She loved her ballet shoes. They made her feel so much like a princess.

7 September

David

It was midnight.
Someone was shouting “Help”.
It sounded like the music box. “It’s so clammy in here. I need some fresh air,” said the voice from the box. It was Sophie the ballerina who lived in the music box. She was trying to push open the lid of the box, but she wasn’t strong enough. Fortunately David the chimney-sweep opened the lid for her.

8 September

Good luck

David wasn’t a real chimney-sweep, he was a doll. Long ago people thought that chimney-sweeps brought good luck, so Aunt Celia had put her lucky chimney-sweep on top of the mantelpiece.
Sophie was very pleased that David was there. He opened the lid of her box every night so that she could be free for a little while.

9 September

Midnight

Aunt Celia didn't know that her dolls came to life. The dolls didn't want her to know. When the clock struck midnight, David leaned his ladder against the wall and strode over to the music box. It was just like a fairytale about a princess and a chimney- sweep in the moonlight.

10 September **Difficult**

"I don't understand how you do it," said David to Sophie. "All day long you dance on one leg. That must be very difficult."
"Yes," nodded Sophie. "A real ballet dancer can balance on her toes for a long time."
"That's amazing!" David thought he would try it himself. However hard he tried, he couldn't balance for more than a count of two on one leg. And he wasn't even standing on pointed toes.
"Never mind," said Sophie as she watched David.
"Chimney-sweeps are not ballet dancers. Besides you haven't got special golden shoes like me."

11 September

Golden shoes

Shoes without buckles,
With no elastic at all,
And shoes without laces
Are the best shoes of all.
They fit as though moulded,
As if they were not there,
Like a part of their own feet
They're what all dancers wear.
The shoes help the dancers
To take steps quite bold.
They really are outstanding,
The ballet shoes of gold.

12 September Knot

David looked down at his boots. Sophie was right. He couldn't dance in great clodhoppers like his. "I know what I'll do," he said. "I'll take them off." He started to untie his laces, but it wasn't easy. David's boots had never been taken off since he was made twenty years ago by the doll-maker. The knots in his laces were really tight. After quite a struggle, he managed to undo the laces on one boot. Now for the other one.

David was concentrating so hard he was sweating. "I think I'll rest a bit before I take this one off," he gasped.

13 September Sky-blue socks

"Yikes. This is hard! " At last, David took off his boot. The boot creaked.

"Oohh, that does feel good," he sighed as he wiggled his toes.

"I never realised you had such lovely socks," Sophie said with admiration.

David looked at them. Sophie was right. They were beautiful sky-blue socks with little red hearts on them.

"I haven't seen these socks for twenty years," David said.

"I'm sure you will be able to dance now," Sophie said and smiled.

14 September **Dirty angels**

Aunt Celia was very neat and tidy. Once a week she cleaned the living room thoroughly.
She fetched a bucket of soapy water and dipped the angel with the harp into it. "Blub blub blub blub!" he spluttered. While he dried out, she cleaned the second angel. The angels didn't like it one little bit.

15 September **Feather duster**

"Ha,ha,ha!" laughed David. The two angels gave him an angry look. He didn't need to laugh at their bad luck. Then they nudged each other. They saw Aunt Celia carrying the feather duster. Because David wore clothes, Aunt Celia didn't wash him. Instead she gave him a good dust.

16 September Tickle

"Help!" screamed David, but it was too late. Aunt Celia had grabbed him. The feathers were long and soft and they tickled like mad. They tickled his neck, his ears, his nose, his mouth, his tummy ...

"Aa .. ah .. tishoo!" sneezed David. He started to scratch. He had an itch in his neck, in his ears, and on his back. One angel said to the other, "I would rather be soaked in the bucket of soapy water than tickled to death with the feather duster."

17 September Sophie's escape

The music box did have its advantages. Music boxes couldn't be put into buckets full of water. Sophie didn't have to have a soapy bath like the angels. And because the box was closed, no dust got in. Aunt Celia therefore only dusted the outside of the music box. Sophie didn't get tickled like David. She felt sorry for the angels and especially for David.

"Tonight, I will scratch his back for him," she promised.

18 September

Stop!

Crick crack turned the key, The music starts to play.
Dance pretty dolly dance, On your golden shoes lead the way.
Just once more,
Come on spin, turn, hop,
Please little dancer
Please don't stop.
Sophie was dizzy,
The world turned before her eyes,
I think that all this spinning,
Really is not wise.

19 September

Dizzy

The twins were spending the day with Aunt Celia. First they played together in the garden. Then they came inside and went to see their favourite music box. The children turned the key, then again and again. Sophie had to keep on dancing. The poor little doll was dizzy. She knew she had got cramp in the leg she pirouetted on.
"Stop it now please!" she cried out in dolls' talk. "Everything is spinning before my eyes."

20 September **I've had enough!**

"That's enough!" shouted Sophie. "I'm not dancing any more!" Nina and Nick had been playing with the music box for hours. Sophie hadn't had a break and she was exhausted. Angrily, Sophie stepped off the stand and laid down.

"Phew, that's better," she puffed.

Nina and Nick were worried. They thought they had broken the music box. Nick quickly closed the lid. Nina anxiously looked at Nick.

"Aunt Celia will be angry."

"I know," said Nick. "But we'll have to tell her." Plucking up their courage, they went to see their aunt.

"Let's go and see," Aunt Celia said, opening the lid of the music box. The ballerina was standing in her usual position. Nina and Nick couldn't understand it. Had they be seeing things?

21 September **Boring**

Sophie and David were sitting on the edge of the mantelpiece. They looked a bit fed up. They were both bored. "Shall we dance?" asked David.
"No, I don't feel like it," Sophie said, shaking her head. David sighed and shrugged his shoulders. Normally Sophie loved to dance. "What's the matter?" David asked her. Sophie pointed to the music box. "That silly thing only plays one tune. It's so dull dancing to the same old tune."

22 September **No imagination**

Oh that silly music box,
It has no imagination.
It only ever plays one tune,
Whatever the occasion.
I cannot dance to just one tune,
That is so very dismal,
I know it off by heart by now,
I find it so abysmal.

23 September **The harp**

The angels on the mantelpiece winked at each other.
They had overheard Sophie the ballerina complaining.
One angel plucked the strings of his harp. Pling, plong. Sophie jumped up.
"Hey angel, can you play the harp?"
The angel nodded his head. "Of course."
"If I ask very nicely, would you play music for me," Sophie asked excitedly.

24 September **Heavenly music**

The angels were playing the harp and the flute. David and Sophie had never heard such wonderful music. It sounded so beautiful and soothing.
David and Sophie glided gracefully across the mantelpiece. They danced as though they were floating on air.
Suddenly David said, "Listening to the angels playing and dancing with you, I feel like I'm in heaven."
"It's quite wonderful, isn't it!" beamed Sophie.

25 September **Trapped**

Aunt Celia was ill. She had been in bed for three days. The dolls didn't realise this though. "I wonder what's wrong?" Sophie was feeling a bit neglected in her music box. It hadn't been opened for three days. Not even at midnight, when her friend David normally let her out. Sophie wanted to get out of the box.
"David!" she cried. "Help me please!" David tried to help her get out, but he couldn't open the box. "It's no good Sophie," he gasped. "The music box is locked and the key isn't in the keyhole!"
"Oh dear! What can I do?" Sophie was desperate.

26 September **Constance Clock**

"Tick, tock, tick, tock," went the clock. "Tick, tock, tick, tock ..." The hands of the clock suddenly stopped moving. "I was afraid of that," said Constance Clock. "I haven't been wound for three days. I knew I would stop. Clocks have to be wound up from time to time." David thought it was eerie without the sound of the clock ticking.
"Hey, Constance, wake up!" he knocked on the case. "Soon no-one will know what the time is!" "There's nothing I can do," moaned Constance. "Without my key, I cannot be wound up, and if I am not wound up my hands won't move."

27 September **Keys**

"I never knew keys were so important," said David. "Without a key, I can't open Sophie's music box and without a key I can't wind up Constance."

The angel with the harp had a suggestion. "Aunt Celia keeps all her keys in a big bunch. Not just the music box key and the clock key, but the key to the front door too. She usually leaves them in the keyhole of the front door."

David needed to get hold of the keys.

28 September **Help from Toby**

David wondered how he could reach the keys. The front door was such a long way off and his legs were so short. "Miaow!" It was Toby, Aunt Celia's big cat. He had heard that David needed the keys to rescue Sophie from her box. "David, I want to help you. I could carry you to the front door on my back," purred Toby. "Really?" Toby wasn't usually so helpful. "Yes," miaowed Toby. "But you must help me too. My cat food is locked up. I haven't eaten for three days. I will take you to the front door if you open the larder door for me." "Okay," David agreed. "It's a deal. Let's go!"

29 September **Thank you**

Toby scampered up to the front door and leapt on to the cupboard next to the front door. He turned round so that his tail faced the lock.

David carefully balanced on Toby's tail. He wobbled a little, but, using all his strength, he grabbed the keys. Crash! The keys fell to the ground.

They raced to the kitchen with the keys to get some cat food for Toby. He was starving. He only had time for a few mouthfuls because David wanted to get back to the mantelpiece.

"Thanks Toby!" David shouted as he turned the key for the music box.

"Thank you Toby!" Sophie smiled as she stepped out of the box.

"Tick, tock Toby!" tocked Constance Clock when David wound her up.

Toby didn't hear them.

His food was more important!

30 September **A kiss**

"You are such a wonderful friend,"
Said Sophie who was in bliss.
"You rescued me in my hour of need,
I reward you with a kiss!"
David blushed crimson red,
But said it was no bother,
We're in this world together,
To help out one another.

1 October

Rain, rain and yet more rain

"Oh what awful weather!" sighed Robert. He was sitting in front of the window. It had been raining all day. Heavy raindrops ran down the window. Robert had a new ball. He would have loved to go outside to play with it, but it was far too wet. He wasn't allowed to play with his ball inside.
He sat and stared out of the window.
"Awful rain, I hate the horrid stuff!" he grumbled.

2 October Come and play

Tring, tring. Neil, Robert's friend, was on the telephone.
"Can you come and play with me?" Neil asked.
"But what will we do? We can't play outside in all this rain," said Robert.
Neil laughed. "But there are lots of things we can do inside.
I know what we can do."
"Oh yes, such as?" Robert wanted to know.
But Neil wouldn't say.
"Come and find out." Robert shrugged his shoulders.
"Okay then. See you soon." He put the 'phone down, then put on his coat and went to Neil's house. He took his football with him, just in case.

3 October Unbelievable!

Neil was Robert's best friend. They both liked the same things. They liked toy cars, animals, and the most important of all – football. They climbed trees. They loved being outside.
So it was a bit strange when Neil said he wanted to play inside. And when he told Robert they were going to play with dolls, Robert was flabbergasted.
Neil got a big box down from the attic. In big black type it said D-O-L-L-S.
Robert didn't say anything. He couldn't believe Neil wanted to play with dolls.

4 October A change of mind

"Are you going to play or not?" asked Neil.
Robert didn't look very enthusiastic. "I'd much rather play football," said Robert.
"But we'll have a fantastic time with these," Neil cried.
Robert wasn't convinced.
Then Neil took a puppet out of the box. Robert was a bit more interested. The puppet was a burglar with a stripy top and a stubbly beard. The puppet was excellent. Robert soon changed his mind. Neil's puppet theatre was great!

5 October

Move your puppet

What a great puppet show,
Grab your doll, here we go.
Move your puppet up and down,
With your fingers make it frown.
Move your thumb to and fro,
Watch its arm, up it goes.
Turn your wrist to the right
Give your friend quite a fright.
Face to face the puppets meet,
Hand to hand they now greet.
It's up to you how they dance,
Now get to it, give it a chance.

6 October

Floppy neck

Robert and Neil were having a great time with the puppets. Robert had never played with puppets before. He wanted to play with the wizard puppet. He tried to get his hand in the puppet, but it was a tight squeeze. He managed it at last. But something was wrong. The wizard's head flopped about. Neil laughed. "Your wizard has got a floppy neck!"

7 October What a lot!

What a lot of puppets Neil had. The boys had found a burglar and a wizard. There was also a Punch and a Judy. There were some more unusual puppets too, such as an Native American Indian with a wonderful headdress. Neil and Robert were unpacking the box of puppets. The afternoon flew by.
"Tomorrow we'll play with the puppets again," they said to each other when it was time for Robert to go home.

8 October A patch on one eye

The puppets were very old. Someone had made the wooden heads and painted them beautifully. Robert liked Burglar Jack best.
"Look," he said, nudging his friend.
"This is a real baddie. He's got a patch on one eye!"
"He really looks evil, doesn't he?" said Neil.
"He would rob people. He'd hide in the woods and then come out at night."

9 October The princess puppet

There weren't just burglars, wizards and witches among Neil's puppets. There was also a princess wearing a golden crown.

"Oh, this is a princess," groaned Neil.

"I'm not interested in her," said Robert. "It's a girl's puppet."

Neil started to act with the puppet princess. "Hello young men," he said in a high-pitched voice. The boys laughed.

Actually it was a very pretty puppet.

10 October Caught you!

Neil and Robert were feeling thirsty.

"Hang on, I'll ask Mummy for some lemonade," said Neil.

He went to the kitchen. Left alone in the room, Robert looked around. He picked up the princess puppet. He thought she was a lovely puppet, but he wouldn't admit it to Neil. He thought she had a lovely face. Robert had to watch out because Neil was coming back from the kitchen. Too late though! Robert blushed.

"Caught you!" laughed Neil

11 October Punch's hat

Robert and Neil had thought of a story that they could act out with the puppets. It was called "Mr Punch's hat".
One day Mr Punch woke up. He couldn't find his hat anywhere. It was because the burglar had stolen it. Punch's hat was made out of material and it had a little bell on the end. Whenever the boys took off Punch's hat, the bell tinkled.

12 October

Punch and Judy

"I'll play Punch," said Neil.
"Right, then I'll play the burglar," said Robert. But there was just one problem. There is always a Judy with a Punch. But neither of the boys wanted to play Judy.
"I'm not a girl!" grumbled Neil.
"Neither am I," groaned Robert.
Neil's mother came to see why they were shouting.
"What's the matter?" The boys explained.
"That's silly!" she laughed. "If you play Judy Neil, then Robert can play a female role too. You could play the witch, Robert."

13 October

The hat

Mr Punch woke up. He had a good stretch and went to fetch his hat. Where was his hat? It had gone! "Judy, have you put my hat in the wash?"

"No," answered Judy, with surprise. "Then someone has stolen my hat!" Mr Punch was horrified. "I bet it was that Burglar Jack!" Punch and Judy searched everywhere for the hat. They followed Burglar Jack's trail until they reached a wood, where the witch lived. "Look," whispered Judy. "There's Burglar Jack with the witch. And there's your hat."

"Aha," said Mr Punch, "and the witch wants to put my hat in her soup!" They came up with a plan. Judy rung the bell at the witch's house and asked if Jack was there. While the witch and Jack were talking to Judy, Punch quickly rescued his hat from the soup cauldron. A happy ending for the story!

14 October **Chinese**

What a strange language,
I understand not a word,
Such different words,
I have never heard.

15 October **Meeting a friend**

Mr Punch met his friend Mr Chow, who was wearing a lovely purple shirt and a red hat. Mr Chow greeted Mr Punch.
"How are you today Mr Punch?" asked Mr Chow
"Well, to be quite honest Mr Chow, I'm on my way to see the doctor."
"Would you like me to come with you?" offered Mr Chow.
"Oh, that would be very kind of you," said Mr Punch.

16 October At the doctor's

"How are you feeling Mr Punch? How can I help?" asked the doctor.
"Well, my eyesight seems a bit blurry doctor."
"Right then," said the doctor. "Could you read out all the letters on the board Mr Punch?"
Mr Punch started off well. He could read all the large letters at thew top and he got down to the bottom line of the board. But these letters were just too blurry. He couldn't make them out at all.
"You've done extremely well, Mr Punch. Perhaps you need some glasses to help you see things that are far away. I think you should see an optician. How about you, Mr Chow? Can you read all the letters?"
Mr Chow could read them all. The only difference was that he did'nt read out the letter 'l'. That was because Chinese people pronounce the letter 'l' like an 'r', but the doctor already knew that.

17 October Princess

Living as a princess
May seem like a bundle of fun,
Yet if you really knew it all,
You would not want to be one.

18 October To the palace

Princess Audrey sighed. She was sitting on her wonderful throne in her wonderful palace and she looked wonderful. She wore the most wonderful clothes, and on her head she had a wonderful crown with the most wonderful pearls in it.
"What's the matter?" the king asked her.
Princess Audrey shrugged her shoulders.
"Nothing Father." But the king could see that his daughter wasn't feeling very happy. He couldn't understand why she was miserable. She had everything her heart desired.
"I tell you what," he suddenly announced.
"I will invite Mr Punch to the palace.
His show will soon cheer you up."

19 October Not funny

Mr Punch put on his best hat, the lovely red one with the golden bell. He was going to the palace. He had to cheer up the princess.

Mr Punch was very excited about his visit to the palace. He couldn't wait to make the princess happy. Off he went. But when he got home later that evening, Mr Punch wasn't so cheerful.

"I don't understand," he groaned. "Princess Audrey didn't like my jokes. She didn't even smile. I couldn't think of anything else to try."

20 October Live an ordinary life

Judy was very sympathetic. "Perhaps the princess is unhappy," she suggested. "There must be a reason why she didn't laugh at your jokes, because they are always funny."

"Unhappy?" exclaimed Mr Punch. "But she lives in a palace with chests full of wonderful clothes and toys and ..."

"Precisely," said Judy. "She lives in a palace full ... of rules. She must always look and behave like a true princess. I've got an idea. Ask her if she would like to come to our very ordinary house, with just one very ordinary chest. Then she can spend an entire day as a very ordinary girl."

"Judy!" cried Mr Punch. "What a good idea! You are absolutely amazing."

21 October

Chattering teeth

Neil and Robert had forgotten about football. They were absorbed in the puppets. Neil had found a green crocodile. The creature had a huge mouth full of very sharp teeth. The crocodile's teeth started to chatter. "Look how cold he is," laughed Neil.
"Daft thing," said Robert. "Crocodiles live in hot places. I have never heard of a crocodile's teeth chattering from the cold!"

22 October **Bite**

I am Coco the crocodile,
I'll bite you in a while,
I'll even bite an elephant's bum,
And watch that I don't bite your tum!

23 October **My trunk**

And I am Ellie the elephant,
I hate creepy things that bite.
If you bite you'd better be quick,
Or with my trunk I'll give you a flick.

24 October Creating voices

Neil and Robert had become skilled puppeteers. They could make the puppets do what they wanted. They had created voices for each of the puppets too.
They were thinking what their Native American Indians might say and do.
"When they attack, they shout 'oowoowoowo'," Robert squealed and used his hand to make the noise over his mouth.

25 October Mr Punch's nose

Robert and Neil were acting out an Indian story. Robert was holding the Indian puppet in one hand and Mr Punch in the other. The story was called 'Mr Punch in the Wild West'. Mr Punch was captured by the Indians when he invaded their land. They tied him up and danced round him. Robert made his puppet dance. To make it more realistic, he wanted to add some Indian war cries too. So he put his other hand over his mouth, but he forgot that he was wearing Mr Punch on the other hand! Mr Punch had a long nose. "Ow!" cried Robert as Mr Punch's nose hit him in the face.

26 October **Dangerous**

"Oh that hurt!" Neil's mother held some cotton wool dipped in cold water on the painful eye. That was better. "I have never heard of anyone being injured by a puppet before," Neil's mother said with a smile.

Robert laughed. "When we play football and go climbing, mum always says 'take care'."

"Well," said Neil's mother, "from now on I'll say 'watch out for Mr Punch, because he is very dangerous'!"

27 October Puppet show

"Do you know what I'd like to do?" Neil said to Robert. "What?" asked Robert.
"Let's give a real puppet show!" said Neil.
"Hey! What a brilliant idea! We can ask all our friends to come and watch," suggested Robert. "Let's do it this Wednesday afternoon when we don't have to go to school."
The two boys started to make plans. "We will need chairs, lots of chairs, just like a real theatre," said Neil.
"No! Children can sit on the floor. Otherwise they'll look into the puppet theatre. And if they see your head," laughed Robert, "that will really scare them."

28 October Scolding

The door bell rang. Mrs Sanderson went to the door, but when she opened it, she was shocked. There were at least twenty children there.
"Oh hello. I'm surprised to see you all," said Neil's mother.
"We have come to see the puppet show," the children told her. Ahhh! Now she understood what was going on. Her son and his friend Robert had invited their friends round to watch a puppet show.
"Come in," she said. She called out to Robert and Neil.

29 October **Thank you**

Neil and Robert went red
and stared at their feet.
"Before you invited all those
children here, you should have
asked me first," she grumbled.
"Yes Mother. I'm sorry,"
squeaked Neil.
"Yes Mrs Sanderson,"
whispered Robert.
Mrs Sanderson could see that the
boys were really sorry.
"Now then, this time ..."
"Thanks mum!"
"Thanks Mrs Sanderson!"
The boys had already rushed to
their puppet theatre.
Mrs Sanderson smiled.
"I think they will all need
a glass of lemonade after
the show," she thought.

30 October **Applause**

Neil and Robert's friends were as quiet as mice. They were watching the puppet show. Neil and Robert were giving quite a performance. Mary Johnson was chewing on her hankie, she found it so exciting. Would Mr Punch catch that terrible burglar? Richard Matthews could hardly sit still. He wanted to help Mr Punch.
"Look out! Behind you! There's the thief!" he screamed at Mr Punch. When the show was over, the curtains dropped and the puppeteers came out from behind the theatre.
"That was excellent," all the children shouted.
"Much better than television," said Richard Matthews.
Had Mary Johnson found it exciting? Well, just look at the hole in her hankie!

31 October

Goodbye

"Goodbye boys and girls until next time,"
Says Mr Punch with a bow.
"Goodbye children, we'll finish with some mime,
Judy will show you how."

"Goodbye Mr Punch and Judy too,
Your show was really great."
Shouts every child, not just a few,
"When's the next show? We can't wait."

The puppet theatre's curtains close,
"More, more," screams every child.
The children all stand on their toes,
The audience is going wild.

1 November

Staying with Grandma

Staying with Grandma was very nice, but all good things come to an end. Billy had already packed his little case. Right ... now into the car. Before he got into the car, his grandma gave him a kiss. “Thank you grandma, see you soon!” he said. “Have you got everything?” asked his grandma. Billy nodded. His sleeping bag, torch, books, pyjamas, toothbrush, and last but not least, Raggy, his rag doll. As they drove off, Father tooted the horn. Billy waved and the car disappeared round the corner.

2 November **Raggy**

Grandma knew it would be quiet in her home without Billy. But hopefully he would be back again next year for a few days. Grandma sighed and went back indoors. Everything was peaceful. There was a gentle breeze blowing through the trees. But what was that lying in the street? It was Billy’s rag doll, Raggy. The doll must have fallen out of Billy’s case when he got into the car. Billy had gone and Grandma had gone back indoors. “Help!” shouted Raggy. “It’s cold and wet here! Billy! Where are you? Please help me!”

3 November

Lunchtime

Raggy the rag doll had spent the morning lying in a puddle. He was wet and dirty. Raggy was getting sadder and sadder. It was time for everyone to leave school for lunch. Raggy could hear shouting and shrieking and the patter of lots of tiny feet dashing home for lunch. Richie had to cross the road. He almost tripped over Raggy. Hey! A doll! His baby sister would love it. He picked up Raggy and took him home.

4 November

Surprise

I have a surprise
For my little sis',
I will give it to her now
With a great big kiss.
Here's a pretty doll for you,
My tiny little tot,
To keep you company and
bring you joy,
As you lay in your cot

5 November **Yuk!**

"Yuck! That doll is disgusting!" Mother wasn't very happy when she saw Raggy. She wanted to throw the doll straight into the rubbish bin, but she saw how upset Richie was at her reaction. "Oh okay, you can keep it!" agreed his mother. "But first that doll goes into the washing machine." She threw Raggy into the washing machine with lots of washing powder. Raggy looked through the round window at the front of the machine. "What's happening?" he muttered to himself. But then ... the whole world started to spin round. "Help! Help!" Raggy shrieked his head off. He coughed and spluttered. His ears, his eyes, his hair, everything was covered in foam. But at least it smelled nice!

6 November **Upside down**

Finally the spinning stopped and Mother took Raggy out of the machine. He was feeling a bit queasy. Richie's mother hung him upside down, pegging his toes firmly to the line. Fortunately the sun was shining and he dried quite quickly. Raggy had a good look round. Clean and dry, he was curious to know where he was. He giggled. "Doesn't the world look funny when it's upside down!"

7 November **Comfy and warm**

Richie's baby sister was really pleased when she saw Raggy. She chuckled and grabbed Raggy with her two little fists.
"Hey!" cried Raggy with surprise. "A bit more gently please!"
After playing with Raggy for a few minutes, she felt quite sleepy. She fell asleep with Raggy clasped firmly in her arms. Raggy thought how different it was to yesterday. Then he was cold and wet on the road and now he was comfy and warm in a cot.

8 November **Screaming**

Richie looked at his little sister. He wanted to see if she was taking good care of his present. Raggy was partly his, he felt, because he had found him abandoned in the street. His little sister was in her play pen. "Where's Raggy?" asked Richie.
His sister chuckled. She couldn't understand what he was saying. Richie noticed two legs sticking out under his sister's bottom. She was sitting on top of the doll! Richie tried to pull Raggy, but his sister wasn't going to let him do that. She started to scream. It was her dolly!

9 November **Pooh!**

Raggy was quite content with his new life. Baby sister sat on top of him sometimes, but she wasn't too heavy! She sucked his feet too, but Raggy didn't mind that it tickled. But there was one thing he didn't like. Baby sister made a mess in her nappy.

"Pooh! It stinks!" Raggy grumbled when baby sister had filled her nappy again.

"Next time Mother washes me and hangs me out to dry, I will pinch one of her pegs. Then I can stick it on my nose!"

10 November **A day out**

Father, Mother, Richie and baby sister were going on for a day out. They were going to the zoo. Mother and Father had packed sandwiches and lemonade and put everything in the car. "Have we got everything?" Mother asked before they set off. Richie and Father nodded. Baby sister held on to Raggy. She was quite content as long as she had Raggy. "Toot toot!" Off they went.

11 November

Best zoo

Hey kids how great,
This picnic is fantastic.
There's so much to see
At the zoo, it is quite frantic.
Will there be a lion or chimp,
A rhino or perhaps a bear?
It's such fun to come here,
It's the best zoo anywhere.

12 November

At the zoo

Raggy was amazed. He had never been to a zoo before. He was sitting in the pushchair and so he had a great view of all the animals. When he saw the lions and tigers he shivered. "Gosh what big teeth they have!" he said. When he saw the giraffes he cried out, "Goodness, what long necks they have!" One of the elephants stuck out his long grey trunk. "Help! He's trying to grab me!" shrieked Raggy. Father moved the pushchair away just in time.

13 November **Sheltered spot**

Time just flies when you are having a good time.
"I'm hungry," Richie moaned. "I'm as hungry as a lion!"
"You are daft!" said his mother and laughed. "Come on then, let's find a nice spot for our picnic. Somewhere sheltered, because there's a bit of a cold wind today."
They found a good spot near the monkeys. They sat on a bench and unpacked the sandwiches and the lemonade.
Father took out a bottle of milk for the baby.

14 November **The monkey**

While the others were eating, Raggy had a little sleep.
He didn't notice that one of the monkeys had crept up to the edge of his cage. It looked through the bars at the strange thing on wheels.
"Hey! There's something in it," said the monkey.
It stretched out its arm through the bar and grabbed Raggy. Raggy woke up with a jolt. "Help!" he screamed. But no-one heard him.
They were too busy eating to notice.

15 November Rescue me?

The monkey had stolen Raggy, but, of course, a monkey doesn't know what stealing is. If a monkey likes something, it grabs it. Off hopped the monkey with Raggy to his bed. It was very dark in the little hut.
"Phew, it stinks! Monkeys smell worse than babies' nappies!" Raggy was so upset. "Isn't someone going to rescue me?" he sighed.

16 November Dodo

Dodo the monkey was in a good mood. She treated Raggy like a baby monkey. She carried Raggy round with her, even to the feeding area. Dodo grabbed a banana and peeled it.
"Here, eat!" She tried to push the banana into Raggy's mouth. Raggy's face was covered with squashed banana. Dodo couldn't understand why Raggy wasn't eating. Bananas were so tasty. She thought Raggy was a stupid baby and threw him up in the air.

17 November High up in a tree

Now poor Raggy hangs
High up in a tree.
He wonders just how long
It'll be before he will be free.
Ten, perhaps twelve monkeys
Climb up to him quite quickly,
The fighting for this small rag doll
Has made them all so prickly.

18 November Squabbling

The other monkeys were squabbling over Raggy. They all wanted to play with him. They pulled his little arms and legs in different directions. It was very painful for poor Raggy.
"Leave me alone!" shouted Raggy.
"I'm only a toy. You shouldn't pull me so hard because you'll rip me!"
The game got wilder. Really it wasn't a game any longer. Each of the monkeys was determined to have Raggy. They shrieked and shrieked.

19 November **Zookeeper**

Tony was a zookeeper at the zoo. He looked after the monkeys. He fed them and kept their cages clean. He noticed that the monkeys in the enclosure had got hold of a doll. "What are you lot up to?" he shouted at the naughty monkeys. "You've pinched someone's doll." He tempted the monkeys to the other side of the cage with a big bunch of bananas so that he could get hold of the doll. Raggy was so pleased to see the zookeeper. "Thank you!" he sighed with relief.

20 November **Lost property**

Tony took Raggy to the zoo entrance. There was an area there for lost property.

"Look what I've found Miss Williams," he said to the woman behind the counter.

"A child must have lost its doll."

"I'll look after it," said Miss Williams. She put Raggy on the floor among the rest of lost property. "Your owner will soon come to pick you up!" she said gently to Raggy.

21 November **Tick tock**

Raggy was sitting between two umbrellas.
At least it was better than the monkey house,
but it was rather quiet.
"Richie's parents will soon come to collect
me!" he mumbled to himself. If he leaned
over, he could just see the clock.
Three o'clock, four o'clock, five o'clock and
still no-one had come to pick him up.

22 November **Still there**

Miss Williams couldn't understand it.
"No-one has come to collect that lovely rag
doll. Surely a child has missed it?" Raggy was puzzled
too. He had been at the zoo for weeks. He had got dirtier
and dustier. Then one evening, Miss Williams put Raggy
in a plastic bag.
"I know someone who will look after you," she said,
as she walked out of the zoo with Raggy.

23 November Alice

Raggy could hear all kinds of sounds - a bus, cars, a door bell and voices. But he couldn't see anything in the plastic bag. Then he heard Miss Williams' voice.
"Is Alice at home?" she asked. Raggy heard footsteps.
"Hello Alice," he heard Miss Williams say. "I've got a dolly here. It has been at the zoo for weeks. Will you look after it?"
"I'd love to!" said Alice. "Even though I've got a hundred dolls, there's always room for one more!"

24 November One hundred and one

Raggy was in Alice's room. Alice had lots of dolls. The were sitting on her bed.
"Hello," said a little clown. "Welcome to the big family!"
"Hello," said Raggy. "Who are you?"
"I am number 89. Alice has so many dolls that she has given us numbers. You are number 101."

25 November

To school

Raggy loved living at Alice's. Sometimes he went with her when she went round to see her friends. Once she took him to school. But she didn't have much time to play with him at school, because she had to study. She had to do sums and learn how to read and write. Raggy thought that if he paid attention to the lesson, he would learn his letters too. At the end of the day Raggy had learned a few letters - **d**, **o** and **l**. When he got back home, he told the other dolls that he could read. "I can read. If you have a d and an o and then two letters l, you have **d-o-l-l**." The other dolls didn't understand it, but they thought that Raggy was very clever.

26 November **Tidying up**

"Come on Alice," said her father, "we are going to tidy up. You can keep ten dolls. The rest are going to the jumble sale." Alice was a bit sad, but she knew her father was right. She chose her ten favourite dolls and the rest had to be packed up in cardboard boxes. Alice was amazed when she saw her tidy room. "Goodness what a big room I've got!" she gasped.

27 November **Dolls' stall**

There was a big toy stall at the jumble sale. Alice's old dolls were there. One of them was Raggy. Raggy was thinking about all the adventures he had had! He was trying to remember them all. He thought about the monkey cage at the zoo, going to school with Alice, being left on the road ... so many adventures, some good and some bad. This was another adventure. Waiting for a new owner.

28 November **Lost and found**

A boy called Billy was wandering around the jumble sale. He was a tall, lanky ten-year-old. He was wearing bleached jeans and a ski jacket. Billy walked past the dolls' stall. He stopped and stared. He picked up one of the dolls.
"Hey Raggy! Do you remember me?" said Billy.
"I lost you a long time ago when I had been staying at Granny's. It's great to see you again!"

29 November **Home**

Billy was delighted to have found Raggy.
He never wanted to lose him again. He got out his money and counted how much he had. He had enough to buy Raggy. The man behind the stall let Billy have Raggy for a good price. Billy took Raggy home. "Welcome home Raggy," he said.
"Do you remember my room?"
Raggy looked around.
Of course he remembered it.
He was back home.

30 November

Never leave you

My sweet little Raggy,
You've been gone for so long,
I won't ever lose you,
It all felt so wrong.
I have missed you so badly
Since you were went away.
I couldn't sleep for ages,
Neither night nor day.
When later in life,
I am fully grown,
I'll make sure my children
Never leave you alone.

1 December

At the baker's

The baker was up very early.
While other people were still
sleeping soundly in their beds, he was
already at work. December was a busy
month for bakers, because they were
getting ready for Christmas. They were
baking biscuits, Christmas cakes and Christmas puddings.
The baker was singing as he made some biscuit mixture. He had
decided to make some gingerbread men.

2 December

Gingerbread men

Bram the baker enjoyed his work. He loved
making gingerbread men, using his own special
recipe. He put all the ingredients into a large
mixing bowl and stirred the rich mixture with his
big wooden spoon.
He rolled out the mixture on his large wooden
table. Then, using his special cutter, he cut out
the gingerbread men. After cooking them in the
oven and then letting them cool,
Bram decorated them with
chocolate drops and icing.

3 December **Tasty foods**

The month of December is the time,
For tasty foods and hot spiced wine.
Who is always first awake?
The baker who must make the cakes,
And all the other delicious things
That the festive season brings.

4 December **Yummy**

Every year at Christmas time, Bram the baker let children visit him to help him make some of his Christmas food. They enjoyed making presents for their friends. They loved making gingerbread men too. They liked to give the gingerbread men names, like Charlie and Harry. But Simon hadn't given his gingerbread man a name. Why not? "Because I've eaten him," he said. "He was yummy!"

5 December In the oven

When the children put their gingerbread men in the oven, their teacher warned them to take care. "Always use oven gloves, because the oven is very hot."
Karen was concerned. "But the heat will hurt our gingerbread men, won't it?"
"No Karen," the teacher reassured her. "Bram has made sure that the oven is just the right heat for your gingerbread men." Alice didn't really believe her. She looked through the glass door of the oven. She was sure her gingerbread man winked at her!

6 December Icing trousers

The gingerbread men were ready.
"We'll just let them cool down, and then you can decorate them," said Bram. Soon all the children had filled their icing bags. They could write or draw with them just like a pen. Tim drew trousers on his gingerbread man. "Mmm," he said, licking his fingers. "I wouldn't mind having trousers made of sugar."

7 December

The snowman

Lots of snow had fallen during the night. The children ate their breakfasts really quickly. They wanted to go out in the snow for a snowball fight and they wanted to make a snowman. They rolled their ball of snow until they had enough for his body. Then they made a smaller ball for his head. They found a big carrot for his nose, two buttons for his eyes and two branches for his arms. He was finished. "Wait a minute!" said David. "He needs a hat and a tie!"

8 December

A talking bird table

The snowman looked at the trees and bushes that were shivering. They didn't like the winter. But Charlie the Great Tit was a winter bird. He didn't mind the cold. He flew over to the snowman. He thought it was a bird table. He started to peck at the carrot. "Hey! Leave my nose alone!" said an angry voice. Charlie almost fell off his perch. "A talking bird table? Whatever next?"

9 December **Cheeky bird**

The snowman was angry with Charlie the Great Tit. That cheeky bird had just pecked holes in his lovely carrot nose. "Buzz off!" he shouted. But Charlie wasn't frightened. He hopped on the snowman's head. "Who are you?" he chirped.

"Surely you can see that I'm a snowman," said the snowman.

"Yes," chirped Charlie. "But what's your name?"

"I don't know. I don't think snowmen have names."

10 December

Strange bird

Charlie said, "Would you like me to think of a name for you?" The snowman thought that was an excellent idea. He couldn't wait to find out what name Charlie had given him. "I know," said Charlie. "Orinoco."

"I've never heard of that name before," said the snowman.

"It sounds impressive, doesn't it?" answered Charlie. "Ideal for a strange bird like you!"

11 December Friends

Charlie the Great Tit visited the snowman every day. Sometimes Charlie brought some friends with him. Robin Redbreast and Bobby Blue Tit had great fun with Orinoco. They played tag around the brim of his hat. Orinoco enjoyed having friends with him. If they got too noisy, he would moan at them. Otherwise they could do what they liked. "It's lovely having friends," he sighed.

12 December

Are you sad?

"What's wrong?" Charlie the Great Tit asked Orinoco. Huge drops of water were dripping from his body.
"Are you sad?" Charlie was worried.
Orinoco sighed. "It's the sun."
Charlie didn't understand. "I tell you what, I'll fetch my friends. They will cheer you up."
Charlie flew off. Silly Charlie. He didn't know that the sun melts snowmen.

13 December **Where are they?**

Charlie the Great Tit had been gone for hours. He had been searching for his friends Robin Redbreast and Bobby Blue Tit. He was sure they would make Orinoco happy.

"Where on earth are they?" Charlie wondered. He searched everywhere – in the park, in the village and even in the woods. Finally he found them on a local farm. They were looking for seeds in the hay.

"Oh, there you both are," gasped Charlie. "I've found you. It's too late to fly to Orinoco now, but in the morning we'll go together."

14 December **Disappeared**

The sun was shining as Charlie the Great Tit, Robin Redbreast and Bobby Blue Tit set off. Charlie had told his friends how sad Orinoco was.

"But where has he gone?" Robin asked, looking puzzled. There was a big puddle where Orinoco used to stand.

"See how much he cried!" said Charlie pointing to the puddle.

"But where is he?" Bobby asked.

The birds searched for ages, but he had disappeared.

15 December

Lapland

In the far north there is a very cold place known as Lapland. Elves live in Lapland. They are very clever elves. They can make anything. That is why Father Christmas uses them to make toys. He needs lots of toys for all the children in the world.

16 December

Presents

The elves liked making presents for Father Christmas. Every year he gave the elves a list of all the presents children wanted.
The chief elf took the list. He scratched his beard and announced, "Today we are going to make dolls."
"Yippee!" cried all the other elves.
They liked making dolls.

17 December Miracle machine

Elf Pour-it-full and Elf Push-the-knob were standing next to a huge machine. They weren't sure how the machine worked. They knew that at one end there was a huge funnel into which one kilogram of pink powder and two kilograms of white powder had to be poured. This was Elf Pour-it-full's job. After he had poured the powder into the funnel, Elf Push-the-knob pushed a knob. The machine began to whirr and buzz and rattle. And wonder of wonders, at the far end of the machine, a doll appeared, and then another, and another. Even the elves gasped in amazement.

"It's a miracle machine," sighed Elf Pour-it-full.

18 December Plop

"Clickety-boom!" goes the machine,
"Clickety-click, clickety-clack,"
The strangest device ever seen,
Look what's coming along the track.
The pink powder starts to cook,
The white is at the simmer,
Hey come and have another look,
There seems to be a glimmer
Of pink smoke rising from the top,
But what's that at the back?
With a plop and then another plop
Dolls appear along the track.

19 December and 20 December **Bare dolls**

Elf Poke-Fun was pushing a trolley full of dolls to the sewing elves. He whistled as he pushed it along. The sewing elves had to make clothes for all the dolls. What was Elf Poke-Fun shouting out?
"Bare dolls for sale! Who wants bare dolls? I have the barest dolls in the world!"
"What nonsense!" scoffed the sewing elves. "Hurry up, then we can get on with our work!"

21 December **Dolls' hair**

The dolls were nearly ready. Elf Brush-on-Paint had painted pretty faces on them and Elf Eye-of-the-Needle and Elf Thimble-Finger had made the most wonderful dolls' clothes. The thing that was missing was the dolls' hair. That was Elf Hair-in-a-Curl's job, but he had a problem. One of the children had asked for a grandma doll. A grandma doll needed grey hair. Where could he find grey hair?

22 December **White beard**

Elf Hair-in-a-Curl had to tell Father Christmas that he couldn't find any hair for the grandma doll. When the elf walked into Father Christmas' room, Father Christmas was snoring. He was snoring so loudly that his beard rose up in the air and flopped down again.

"What a lovely white beard? That would be just the thing for our grandma doll!" Elf Hair-in-a-Curl smiled and fetched his scissors. Very carefully he snipped off a few strands of Father Christmas' beard.

23 December A few baubles

Our Christmas tree this year
Has not a single ball,
Father had just fetched the box,
When he slipped and let it fall.
Our tree is not a pretty sight,
Except for all the lights,
If only we had a few baubles,
To make it full and bright.

24 December Accident

"I'm afraid there has been an accident," said Father sadly. "I dropped the box with all the Christmas decorations. I'm afraid they're in pieces." Peter and Lizzie were really disappointed. Hanging the decorations on the Christmas tree was such a treat. Father felt very guilty, but what could he do? He had an idea. He took them into the kitchen and said, "This year we're going to make pretty decorations for the tree. We'll hang them on the tree very soon." "Yippee," shouted Peter and Lizzie. "That's a great idea!"

25 December

New decorations

Peter and Lizzie were making figures and shapes to hang on the Christmas tree. They made dwarfs and elves, shepherds and angels, bells and birds out of dough. Then they cooked them in the oven until the dough was really hard. After they had cooled, they painted them. When the paint had dried, they made little ties and tied the Christmas decorations on the tree.

"Doesn't the tree look pretty?" cried Peter.

Lizzie agreed. "I like the decorations more than the ones Daddy dropped."

26 December **Keeping warm**

The crib was under the Christmas tree. The ox and the ass looked into the stable. Joseph and Mary stood beside the cradle where baby Jesus laid.
"The poor child," said the ox, "without any clothes."
"Yes," agreed the ass, "And not even a blanket to keep him warm." The ox and the ass decided that they would have to do something about it. They had to find something to keep the child warm. The ass climbed on the back of the ox so that he could reach the Christmas tree.
Using his teeth, he plucked some hair from an angel.

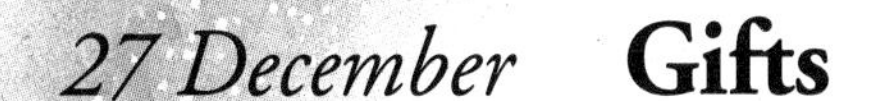

27 December **Gifts**

The three kings had brought a gift to the baby Jesus in his crib in the stable – gold, frankincense and myrrh. Mary and Joseph thanked the kings.
"We have been given so much!" they said.
"Wait a moment!" they heard voices outside the stable. It was the ox and the ass.
"We have a present too," shouted the ox.
"A warm blanket of angel hair," brayed the ass.
"Picked from the Christmas tree."

28 December **A fine present**

Mary and Joseph were so pleased.
They had received so many gifts, even a present from the ox and the ass too.
"How kind of you," Mary said softly.
The ox and the ass blushed with pride.
"Oh, it's only a little thing," mumbled the ox shyly.
"Well ..." sighed the ass. "It's not a real present from a shop. We just plucked some angel hair from the Christmas tree."
Joseph shook his head. "That's not the point. You thought about what our child needed. It is finer than the most extravagant gift ."

29 December **Albie**

Albie was a teeny tiny doll. On his teeny tiny head he wore a teeny tiny hat. Between his teeny tiny eyes he had a turned-up nose that made him look very cheeky. He wore teeny tiny clogs on his teeny tiny feet. He was always looking for adventure. He walked around only at night when people had gone to sleep. "Clickety-clack, clickety-clack" went his teeny tiny clogs.

30 December

The moon and the stars

Albie was sitting on the windowsill. It was the middle of the night. He looked at the moon. "It looks like there's a man in the moon!" he gasped. "I would love to go and visit him and all the stars too. Look how many stars there are. It could take me years and years to visit them all!"

31 December

Journey to the moon

Ten, nine and then eight,
It is still not too late!
Seven, six and what's more,
Next comes five and then there's four.
Three, then two and now it's one,
And after one the New Year's come.
Time for all to celebrate,
But what will be teeny Albie's fate?
Has he got an earthly chance?
See the New Year fireworks dance,
As strapped on board a rocket soon,
He makes his journey to the moon.